MURDER BUNNY AND THE CARROT CAKE CAPER

A Cozy Mystery

HANNAH DOVE

ISBN (electronic): 978-1-960936-65-3

ISBN (print): 978-1-960936-66-0

CONTENTS

Chapter One

AGNES

"Agnes Brooms, what are you still doing here?"

Agnes jumped at the loud voice, so unusual for the library. She stepped back, almost knocking over the bookshelf behind her, face springing out of the novel to see the head librarian, Esther Seawell, coming towards her.

Reacting to the chastisement and not registering the words, Agnes slammed her book closed. She'd been returning it to the shelf, but the image of a black cat on the cover had caught her eye and she'd peeked inside. It wouldn't have been the first time Esther had caught Agnes reading on the job.

"Didn't I give you the afternoon off?" Esther said, voice lowering as she got closer.

Agnes looked down, feeling guilty all of a sudden. "There's a lot to do here."

"Pish posh," Esther scolded her. "The library's empty, and I can't afford to pay you if you work overtime. Why don't you head down to the fairgrounds?"

Most people in Warrenton would be at the fairgrounds today. Though the annual festival was still a week away, preparations had already begun, and today was the preliminary for the baking competition. The Warrenton Bake-Off was the fair's most popular event, with the winner receiving the coveted Golden Spoon trophy and, more importantly, bragging rights. Almost everyone in the town entered, so the preliminary contest whittled down the competitors to a manageable five individuals.

Every year, Agnes had gone to the preliminary and the festival with her grandmother. Dolores Brooms had been an exceptional baker, and the Golden Spoon had graced her kitchen for quite a few years.

With her grandmother gone, however, there was no chance of that happening again. Agnes had considered entering herself this year. She'd always loved watching her grandmother bake, but the talent didn't seem to have been passed on. She'd tried some raspberry cinnamon cookies, which was a questionable choice to begin with, and they'd come out so horrible that even her Uncle Curtis hadn't stolen them when he came by to raid her fridge.

"Why don't you head down for a change?" Agnes suggested. While there was part of her that felt sad to miss the contest, the idea of going felt painful. "You wouldn't need to pay me overtime, and it could be fun for you."

Esther wrinkled her nose, her thin lips pulling down. "It's not much fun for a diabetic."

Oh dear, Agnes felt guilty for forgetting that Esther had diabetes. Part of what made the preliminaries so popular was that the townspeople voted for who should compete in the finals. Competitors offered their desserts for free, hoping that whoever tasted it would give it a good score.

Esther sighed and reached over, resting a thin hand comfortingly on Agnes' shoulder. "I know it must be different for you without her dear, but she'd have wanted you to go. And I'm sure you have friends competing who you ought to support. Mr. Davies will be there won't he?"

"Well, yes," Agnes admitted. She wouldn't exactly call her neighbor, Nigel Davies, a friend. He was a portly British man who had moved to Warrenton a few years back and set up an antique shop. He lived on the floor above it, right next to Agnes' house. Nigel was pompous and curmudgeonly, with his most humanizing trait being the affection he showed for the fluffy white rabbit that had accompanied him from England.

For all his flaws, however, there was no denying that Nigel was an excellent baker. He'd won the Bake-Off last year with his black currant scones. It had caused quite the commotion, with contestants and watchers alike questioning the judges decision. They'd had to distribute some among the crowd to get everyone to quiet.

This year, Nigel had chosen a more traditional dessert. It was rumored that he'd spent the past year working on his carrot cake recipe, and Nigel swore that this cake was certain to win him the trophy once again.

Since Agnes wasn't a judge for the official contest, this was probably her only chance to taste it. Nigel hadn't let anyone taste it yet, and he certainly wouldn't offer any to Agnes after the contest.

"You can't hide away in the library forever," Esther continued, patting Agnes' shoulder before crossing her arms. She tilted her head forward and peered over the tops of her spectacles, shooting Agnes the stern, lecturing look she reserved for misbehaving teenagers. "It was sweet of you to stay here while you were looking after Dolores, but you're not in your twenties anymore. It's time for you to get out there and start living your life. You need to have your own adventures."

Agnes returned the novel she was holding to its rightful place on the shelf. She wasn't sure that going to the preliminaries of a baking competition qualified as an adventure. If anything, the library was more exciting. The room itself was boring and its old furniture could have used an upgrade, but books gave Agnes access to more adventures than could ever have been available in a little town like Warrenton.

It seemed a clever argument, and Agnes turned to Esther, planning to make it. However, the words died on her lips before she'd had a chance to utter them. There was a reason that none of the kids in the library ever talked back to Esther. The older librarian was intimidating with her tall, thin frame, frowning lips and eyes that could glare a hole into you when she peered over the tops of her glasses.

With a sigh, Agnes gave in to her boss and grabbed her coat. "I promise to be in early tomorrow."

"I'd rather you didn't," Esther said, but she laughed good-naturedly. "Now, out the door, you."

Agnes left the library and drove over to the fairgrounds in the little old bug that she'd inherited from her grandmother. On the way, she admitted to herself that Esther might have been right to send her out. Maybe she *had* been hiding in the library. Things had gotten so hard for her after her grandmother died. Everyone in the town praised Agnes for staying and caring for Dolores, but the truth was just the opposite. It was her grandmother who had been taking care of her, and without her, Agnes felt overwhelmed by the responsibilities of being entirely on her own.

Agnes parked her car and walked over to the fairgrounds. At first, they seemed the same as usual. She saw a group of teenage girls whispering in a corner together. The recently widowed Dr. Michaels was pressed against a tent being bombarded by single mothers. In another area, Lilah Dorchester, the hospital's head nurse, was desperately trying to get people to try her brownies.

Agnes narrowed her eyes. That did seem odd. Lilah could be pretentious at times, but her brownies were delicious. It wasn't the norm for her to have trouble finding takers.

At another booth, already packing away a rather gelatinous looking cheesecake, Agnes spotted her friend, Cindy, who'd appeared to have taken extra time styling herself that morning. Instead of its usual quick ponytail, Cindy had curled her hair into blonde ringlets that gave her round face an extra-girlish appearance. She'd tied a floral apron over her jeans and loose blouse.

Agnes headed towards her friend.

"I didn't know you'd entered this year," Agnes said, trying to keep the jealousy out of her voice. She wished she had the skills even to try. "Let me have a taste? I'll give you a good score."

"Aggie?" Cindy asked looking up. She gave Agnes a friendly smile before her lips tilted in a frown. "It's sweet of you to offer, but I don't think there's much point."

"Just because you don't make it to the competition doesn't mean you shouldn't try," Agnes pointed out, though she hadn't been brave enough to take her own advice.

"No, it's not. Well, I don't think I'd have made it to the competition anyway, but I'm pretty sure the preliminaries aren't happening today after all."

That caught Agnes off guard. The preliminaries were always the Sunday before the festival. "What do you mean?"

"You haven't heard yet, have you?" Cindy's shoulders slumped, and she leaned forward to whisper the rest to Agnes, the way one might when delivering particularly unpleasant news. "It's poor Mr. Davies. He dropped dead."

Chapter Two

AGNES

It took a few seconds for the news to sink in.

Agnes stared at Cindy, eyes wide. Mr. Davies couldn't be dead. She'd seen him just earlier that morning, locking up his store. "What happened?"

"I don't know, but supposedly Marie found the body, and you know how she is." Cindy rolled her eyes. "She's lying on a massive stuffed lion in one of the tents. Says she can't breathe due to how traumatizing it was, though she's managed to get the word out to a lot of people."

Agnes and Cindy had both been in class with Marie from elementary to high school. She was nice enough, but she had a flair for the dramatic. She'd made it through to the Bake-Off last year, but burst into tears when Nigel won.

"But what happened to him?" Agnes asked. "Nigel, I mean?"

Cindy shrugged. "The police came by a few minutes ago. I guess they'll be able to say."

Agnes turned in the direction that Cindy was looking, towards the large silver ring. It was missing its seats still, but in a week, the Ferris wheel would be functional. "He was by the rides?"

"I heard it was close to the merry-go-round. Are you going to see, Aggie? It'll be madness over there!"

"I know, but it just seems so bizarre." Agnes couldn't explain her desire to see the body. Maybe it was to convince herself that Nigel was really dead, or maybe it was because Esther had told her that she needed more adventure.

"Well, good luck," Cindy said. "Let me know if you see Marie. Bet she's a sight."

Agnes gave Cindy an amused chuckle before setting off. She waved to some of the other townspeople as she passed, but there were more people she didn't recognize. The festival attracted crowds from all around the state so that, for a couple weeks a year, Warrenton overflowed with thousands of tourists.

Sunlight reflected off the bright paint of the half set-up carnival rides. A large, balding man stopped setting up the tracks for the children's train long enough to stare up at Agnes with a large glass eye. He scowled at her, or maybe it was a smile. Either way, she waved back uncomfortably before increasing her pace.

Finally, she saw the smiling face of a pink horse, ready to run circles around the carousel. It wasn't hard to locate the body from there: A large crowd had gathered around a tent with a British flag on top of it. Nigel had brought the tent last year as well. He hated the sun.

Agnes pushed her way into the crowd. Many of the strangers shot her annoyed glares, but a few townspeople recognized her as Nigel's neighbor and helped her move forward.

A couple of policemen were stationed outside of the tent's flaps, holding their arms out and trying to keep the crowd at bay. Agnes knew the younger of the pair. His name was Evan

Wilson, and she used to babysit him. She couldn't believe he was old enough to be a police officer now.

"Evan," she called to him, waving at him as she pushed past a particularly robust man. "Is it Nigel?"

The young policeman looked startled at the sound of his name. He turned and spotted Agnes, and his face relaxed. He glanced at his partner before stepping closer to her.

"Yeah, it is. He was your neighbor, right?"

Agnes nodded. He had a good memory. "What happened to him? He seemed fine this morning."

"Coroner's in there now, but it looks like a heart attack."

Agnes couldn't believe it. Nigel was rotund, but he'd always seemed healthy. "He was barely in his fifties."

Evan nodded in agreement though Agnes imagined that to him, fifty sounded old. "Do you have any ideas about next of kin, Aggie? We're not sure who to call."

Agnes shook her head. Nigel was a bachelor and the rest of his family were in England. "I know he has a sister. I think her name was Fiona. Her number might be in his phone, but I can't tell you."

"No, that's helpful stuff, really. Thanks." He smiled in appreciation before crossing to his partner. He tapped his shoulder and told him what Agnes had said. The partner nodded, and then Evan slipped into the tent.

Agnes licked her lips, debating whether to leave. She hadn't seen Nigel's body, but she wasn't sure she needed to anymore. The reality of his death was sinking in, and standing in a sweaty crowd in the hot sun no longer seemed like much of an adventure.

Just as she was preparing to make an escape back through the throngs, Evan stepped back out of the tent. He held a crate in one of his hands.

Agnes turned her head, trying to see what was inside, but she could guess. "Is that Nigel's rabbit?"

"It is."

"Where are you taking him?"

"Poor guy's got to go to the shelter," Evan said, glancing down at the cage. "Don't imagine Nigel's family is going to fly here to collect him. But he's adorable. I'm sure someone will want him."

Agnes felt a sudden sadness wash over her. The bunny had lost his owner and now he was going to a shelter? Evan sounded optimistic, but Agnes doubted there was a large market for adult rabbits, even long-haired white ones from England.

Evan started making his way out the crowd, which reluctantly parted as they saw his uniform. The crate in his hand swung, turning towards Agnes.

When she looked down at it, she saw the bunny. Inside the crate, its face was staring out at the crowd with large brown eyes.

Its gaze turned to Agnes, and for a second, she swore its eyes widened and its ears pricked up, almost as though it were a human who had just had an idea.

Chapter Three

MURDER BUNNY

Goodness gracious, this day has been horrific.

Yet it started out so positively that I can't quite make heads or tails of it.

I saw Nigel, my now-dead owner, wake up this morning feeling very enthusiastic about the qualifier round of the baking competition.

I watched him closely, as is my habit. He paced around the kitchen in his lavender terry cloth bathrobe, a mud mask on his face, going on and on about how he was certain to sail through the qualifier, about how the world wasn't ready for his newest recipe. He was right. Nobody was ready for that recipe. Nigel had come up with the greatest carrot cake that I'd ever nibbled.

And that's saying a lot, since I'm a bunny.

Anyways, Nigel carried on and on about cream cheese frosting, commitment to one's art, and how the most precious commodity in this world was enthusiasm. Nigel was always rambling on like that. He loved to address me, asking questions and then answering them. As usual I said nothing.

I've found it's better to play stupid in the company of humans.

Everybody wants a dumb bunny.

Anyways, he was all a bit too much for me. As the rant continued, I hunched down in the corner of my hutch, nibbling on my morning watercress and scented lemon water, listening. The one good thing I will say about Nigel is that he always kept me stocked in the very best food and beverage.

I'll miss that about him.

At noon he emerged from his bedroom fully dressed in his white baker's outfit. I ran circles around the hutch for a few seconds, pretending to be excited. We have to embarrass ourselves, us bunnies, to keep a roof over our heads.

"Fluffy, if you continue behaving yourself, someday I'll let you inside my bedroom." He crouched down and peered at me. I could see the cream glistening on his mustache. "But until then, it's not for animals, no matter how cute." His finger jabbed at me through the squares of the cage, and my nose twitched involuntarily. I hate it when that happens.

It's both funny and sad that Nigel assumed I'd never seen his bedroom. Even given his posh British accent, with his plummy vowels and endless wit, he never figured out that I could open my cage. He never noticed the bits of pine shavings that I inevitably tracked out when I went out for my late-night adventures in his home. Maybe he'd mistaken me for a silly Pomeranian.

Again, everybody wants a dumb bunny. So that's what I give them.

Nigel removed his recipe book from the cupboard and lay it gingerly upon the table. The recipe book had a combination lock on it, if you can believe that. He only opened it when nobody was around, and kept it locked and shelved at all other times.

Of course, I'd sussed out the four-digit combination long

ago. You never know when you might need to know some-thing like that.

I watched him lay the book out on the countertop and dial the combination and open it up.

"And so it begins," he announced to nobody. I watched him begin to assemble the ingredients. Flour, sugar, butter, eggs, carrots, vanilla essence. A series of unmarked containers with mysterious ingredients that his pudgy fingers handled with reverence. It was all a mystery to me.

But I had faith in Nigel. He'd worked for months on this carrot cake recipe, and he had the track record to prove it.

Next, he pulled the cover off his red KitchenAid mixer and ran a loving finger along its edge. Nigel guarded the machine like a national treasure and spent many evenings cleaning it.

I curled up in my wood shavings and started to read the paper. You humans assume I can't read because I'm a bunny, but what you don't realize is that I've spent most of my life living on top of newspapers. They line the bottom of my cage, beneath the pine shavings, and I've learned about every-thing that you can learn from a newspaper, from news to sports to politics to lifestyle to weather to advertisements.

Nigel started the mixing, using both hand and machine. "See, Fluffy, what they don't know is that the texture starts at the beginning. It's the combination of the two." Later, he lovingly poured the batter into three different cake pans and massaged them with his silicone spatula. He slid the pans into the preheated oven and paced the kitchen while it baked, the sweet aroma of ginger and carrot floating through the air.

When the kitchen timer rang, Nigel sprang towards the oven. He removed the cakes, let them cool for exactly six minutes on the counter. Then he began assembling the finished product, handling the disks with great care, gently smoothing the cream cheese frosting between the layers, and finally coating the entire cake.

When it was finished, he removed a small box from a cupboard. He opened it and gingerly removed an item from a small box, only a few inches high. "Now for the finishing touch," Nigel said. "The topper. This cake is going to win me the competition for the sixth time in a row."

It looked like a small bell tower. He gently placed it on top of the cake. Then he backed away and rubbed his hands together.

"I am the best," he said.

I twitched a skeptical whisker.

"What? It's not bragging if it's true."

Half an hour later, the cake was boxed up and in Nigel's car. He had put on his trenchcoat and begun humming to himself. I didn't know his intention, but I wasn't going to let him leave without me. I'd traveled with him to the fair each of the last five years. I'd suffered the fingers of pink frosting thrust into my hutch, the bits of oatmeal cookie that children dropped onto my back from above.

Spending a week at the county fair wasn't my cup of tea, but I refused to be left alone. He didn't know it, but Nigel needed me.

Drawing in my breath, I stood up on my hind legs, gripped my cage with my paws, and rattled it using every ounce of my strength.

Nigel stopped in the doorway and turned. "What's that, Fluffy? You want to come?"

Fluffy. The name made me nauseated. I never liked that diminutive. Still, I began leaping, just to make my intentions clear.

"Well, that's a surprise." He stroked his chin. "I thought that you didn't enjoy the fair last year."

I shook the cage harder, then did a cute flip.

Nigel sighed. "All right, I suppose you could come this year." He picked up my crate by the handle and carried me outside.

I was quite fond of Nigel. He usually did what I wanted.

————

At the fair, Nigel got a couple of the local kids to set up the tent in exchange for some biscuits he'd made. He wasn't going to waste his carrot cake on them. Wise. Children have no appreciation for good food. Sticky little creatures think anything with enough sugar is delicious.

Nigel rested my hutch down in the corner of the tent and began setting up his cake station in the center. Today was all about flavor, but Nigel was a showman. He'd brought a stand and even a set of tiny lights. He loved a good presentation and said that it was the reason for his win.

One by one, people trickled over while he was preparing his cake. I recognized a few of them. They'd be competing with Nigel in the contest. A lot of them offered him some of their own foods to try. I could tell from the look of triumph on his face and the condescending compliments that none of their desserts could approach the magnificence of Nigel's carrot cake.

As they chatted, I lay in my hutch, watching their feet and waiting for the cooing to begin. Sure enough, it did. *Oh my look at him.* Then: *What a beautiful little creature!* Finally: *Be careful or he might end up on my plate!* I twitched my whiskers and pretended to giggle at that one. You have no idea how many times I've been sweetly threatened to end up on somebody's plate.

The crowd died down. The occasional person would come in and speak with Nigel, but I paid it little attention. There was a lump of frosting stuck on my ear. No amount of scratching with my paw seemed to be getting it off. It was driving me crazy and keeping me quite preoccupied.

That's when I heard a thump, and then a cry.

Nigel had fallen over, onto the ground. I couldn't see his face but something was definitely wrong. I don't know if he was breathing or not.

I wondered if I ought to break out of my cage and go for help, but I saw another pair of feet. There was another human in the tent. I assumed they would sound an alarm or call for help of some kind, whatever it was humans did when someone suddenly fell to the floor clutching their chest.

The feet vanished, and I waited. Surely, someone would come soon.

It was a few minutes before another pair of feet appeared. I heard a girl calling Nigel's name. She screamed.

————

The next hour was a flurry of activity. I saw legs, calves, and feet, but I couldn't see Nigel through the crowd. I heard the anxious voices conferring closely. By the time the paramedics arrived, I began running in frantic circles in my cage, but nobody noticed me. Dumb bunnies get forgotten. I watched them put Nigel on a stretcher and wheel him away.

Then a pair of black police shoes arrived next to my cage. "We'll have to take this bunny to a shelter of some kind," said a male voice. "It doesn't seem like Nigel has anyone in the area to take him."

"A shelter?" said another voice. "Could as well just let him free, y'know? The shelter's only going to end up putting him down."

My ears went flat. I felt the panic rising in my haunches. Did I get a say between those two options? Because I definitely chose freedom. I began to run in circles trying to communicate this choice. I didn't know what else to do. Sometimes it worked, sometimes it didn't.

They weren't looking at me.

"Don't say that," the first man said. "He'll be fine. The animal shelter's not that bad."

Then my cage was lifted up. I saw the humans. They didn't stare at me like I was used to, however. They were too busy examining the tent. I looked around and spotted Nigel's display table. The lighting, the decorations, and the cake stand were all there.

However, the carrot cake that Nigel had spent the morning obsessing over had vanished.

The officer kept carrying my crate, taking me out of the tent. I didn't have time to dwell on the missing cake.

I could feel my heart thumping. This was very bad. I had to deal with one problem at a time. I couldn't survive in an animal shelter. They'd toss me in a little crate with a bunch of other rabbits. They'd feed me pellets. I'd have to tolerate the dumb bunnies' dumb conversation. It would be torture.

In the midst of my panic, I gazed out at the crowd of humans around Nigel's tent. That was when I saw her.

A young woman wearing a conservative yellow gingham print dress. It had a ruff around the neck. Her dark hair was cut in a conservative bob and her fingers were interlaced around a small clutch. Her eyes were large and sensitive and even a little watery. She looked like someone who needed a bunny.

And she was looking at me.

I had to act fast. I flipped my body around and kicked open the cage door. I knew exactly how to make it look like an accident. Then I leaped out onto the ground and hopped straight over to the woman. I sat on her shoe and leaned my head against her shin and began trembling.

"Oh my goodness," she said.

"He likes you, Agnes," said the police officer. He came over and looked down at me. I was really shivering now. It wasn't easy to look this vulnerable but I knew that my future depended upon it.

"I'm unsure about what to do."

"Agnes, would you be willing to take care of Nigel's bunny for a while?" he said.

She looked down at me. I looked up at her. Our eyes met.

"Yes, I suppose I will," she replied.

Chapter Four

AGNES

On the drive home, her eyes checking the bunny's crate in the backseat, Agnes started to doubt her decision. What had she just done? Could she handle the responsibility of taking care of an animal? She could barely take care of herself. And she didn't know anything about this rabbit. What did it eat? Where would it sleep? Had it been inoculated?

She took a deep breath. She was being ridiculous. Of course, Nigel would have gotten the rabbit vaccinated. It had come over with him from England, and Nigel hadn't been the type to forget something vital like that.

Still, the other questions were real concerns. Agnes had never had a pet before. Her grandmother thought animals were too much stress, and Agnes forgot to feed herself sometimes when she got distracted.

Agnes parked her car in front of her house and lifted the bunny's carrier out of the backseat. It was heavier than she expected, and the animal hopping around inside made it awkward to hold. Agnes felt the acute lack of strength in her arms. Holding a rabbit was not like stacking library books.

Afraid she might drop it, Agnes rested the crate onto the grass. She looked down at the bunny. It looked up at her, almost as if waiting for her to speak.

"What is it?" she said.

The bunny said nothing.

"Do you want something? Maybe a carrot?"

It ran around the crate in an agitated circle. For a moment, Agnes thought that he could understand her. That was ridiculous. Of course a rabbit couldn't understand her. That was her overactive imagination.

Agnes lifted the crate again, this time holding it steady with both her hands. It was easier that way, though she struggled again when she got to her porch and pushed through her front door. There, she nearly dropped the bunny in surprise.

Uncle Curtis was sitting on the couch, shoes off and clipping his toenails on the coffee table. His large gut crept out from beneath the bottom of his stained t-shirt.

Agnes groaned. The last thing she needed was another territorial dispute.

"Oh, hey Aggie." He nodded at her, as though it were perfectly normal for him to come home and find him trimming his nails on her couch. "Buy yourself a cat finally?"

Agnes paused for a second as she was putting down the crate. What was that supposed to mean?

She glanced at the bunny. It almost looked like his eyes had narrowed and he was glaring at her uncle. She was certain she was imagining the expression, but it made her smile all the same.

"What are you doing here, Uncle Curtis?" she asked, putting her hands on her hips and trying to look commanding. "Grandma kicked you out."

"But she never changed the locks." He grinned as he cut his final toenail with a loud snap. Agnes waited to see if he would brush them off the table now that he'd finished, but he didn't. He stood and stretched his arms. "Anyway, I'm sure she'd have let me back in eventually. So, what's for dinner?"

"Nothing," she said. "And you can't just come in here any more. It's *my* house. Grandma left it to me. You have your apartment."

Her uncle scowled. "That place? Yuck. No. Too small and too smelly. There's dirt everywhere."

Whose fault was that? The apartment would have been neither dirty nor smelly if Uncle Curtis bothered to clean it, but he did not. Her uncle's laziness had been a source of great distress to her grandmother while she'd been alive. He'd spent most of his adult life floating between odd jobs and mooching off his mother. Last year, Grandma had enough and kicked him out of the house, though she'd been nice enough to allow him to stay in the apartment she owned a few blocks away.

Agnes kept glaring at him. She even tried tapping her foot and frowning the way her grandmother used to, but it was no use. Short of calling the police, she wasn't certain how she was going to get her uncle to leave.

"Wow, Aggie—that's a weird cat you've chosen, isn't it?" He pointed to the floor beside her feet.

Agnes looked down and her eyes opened in surprise. The rabbit had come out of his crate and was hopping along the floor.

Had Agnes not closed the carrier properly when she'd placed him inside? Or was there a flaw in the locking mechanism? He'd managed to escape at the fairgrounds as well.

"It's Nigel's bunny," Agnes explained to her uncle. "He's dead. Something happened to him at the fair."

"Someone finally offed the pompous jerk?" Uncle Curtis chuckled.

Agnes crossed her arms. She hadn't been friendly with Nigel either, but that was going too far. He might have looked down on the other townspeople a bit, but he hadn't been a bad person. "I believe it was a heart attack."

"Well, this creature is certainly excitable, isn't he?" Her uncle chuckled as he watched the bunny.

The white rabbit was hopping across the wooden floorboards with a fierce determination to its bounces, as though it had a specific destination in mind. In this case, it seemed like it was trying to get to Uncle Curtis.

Agnes recalled how the bunny had made a beeline towards her at the fair. She'd wondered if he'd recognized her somehow. She had been into Nigel's antique shop on quite a few occasions. It wasn't impossible that the animal recognized her uncle as well.

"I think he likes me," her uncle said, leaning over and reaching a hand towards the bunny as it approached him. "You want to hang out with me, little fella? Ow!"

The rabbit had bit his finger.

Agnes covered her mouth, trying to suppress a giggle, as her uncle recoiled his hand, shaking it wildly in front of him.

"That thing's a demon!" he said. "It shouldn't be around people."

He went to kick the bunny, which managed to dodge his foot. Agnes rushed forward and grabbed the rabbit, lifting it to safety in her arms before her uncle managed a successful attempt.

"I promised I'd keep him for at least a little while," Agnes said. The bunny fussed in her hands for a few seconds, but she held it tight and it eventually settled. "He'll be staying here in *my house*."

Uncle Curtis narrowed his eyes. Agnes was worried he would argue with her for a second, but he glanced at the kitchen and let out a loud huff. "Fine. Doesn't look like you made dinner anyway."

He gave the rabbit one last angry glare before sauntering out of the house.

Agnes breathed a sigh of relief as he left. She really needed to change those locks.

Chapter Five

MURDER BUNNY

The next night I sat in my crate, in its new home on the kitchen floor, and watched Agnes as she read her third book of the evening.

She was in the living room, curled up on her antique Queen Anne sofa with a multicolored afghan strewn across her legs. On a small table, steam rose from a chipped floral cup of tea. All around her rose stacks of old hardcover books. Many of them looked like they'd been purchased at a library used book sale, which in fact they had. Those library book sales were a real weakness.

Agnes set her book down and blew her nose into a tissue. "My heavens, I'm tired." She sipped her tea, then spit it out. "This is still much too hot. Goodness, nothing is going right today."

I remained completely still. The only sound was of a ticking grandfather clock. I wanted to see if she would remember her most important task of the day.

Suddenly Agnes looked over at me. "You must be hungry," she said.

There it was. I did a little hop in my cage, just to let her know that she'd guessed right.

"I swear you understand me," she said, rising from the sofa. "I bought you something special at the store today."

Oh boy. I wondered what it could possibly be.

She went to the refrigerator and opened the vegetable drawer and removed a large plastic bag. I recognized the contents immediately. It was the least surprising thing, the bane of my existence.

"Carrots," she said. "That's what bunnies eat, don't they?"

No, I wanted to scream, *that's not what bunnies eat*. I hate carrots. They are cheap and stupid and they require no imagination to prepare. There are at least twenty other vegetables that we like more than carrots. Ask anybody who's owned one of my kind. They'll tell you that most of us like to eat high-quality hay.

Me, I'm a bit more refined. It's watercress or nothing on my dinner plate. But the only person in the world who knew that was dead, and I didn't know how to communicate my preference to Agnes without revealing my secret.

"I'm going to make it easier for you to eat," she said. I watched her cut three carrots into six halves and place them into a dish. Then she opened my crate and set them down before me.

"Enjoy," she said.

I turned my back on her.

"Are you saying you don't like carrots?"

This was good news. She would be trained quickly.

"Well what do you prefer? The pet store was closed by the time I got there after work today."

I waggled my powder-puff tail, not knowing what else to do.

"Maybe if I leave them here, you'll eat them."

That was wrong, wrong, wrong. I have good taste and she

needed to understand that from the outset. While Agnes closed the gate and rose to her feet, I picked up one of the half-carrots with my teeth, carried it to the wire mesh, and pushed it out of the crate. It fell onto the kitchen floor. *Thump.*

"Oh my goodness!" she said. "You really don't like carrots, do you?"

Just to emphasize my point, I did it again with a second half-carrot. *Thump.*

"Okay, I get the point." She crouched down and opened the crate and removed the carrots. Then she paused, looking at my bedding. Her fingers pushed some of it aside. "Is that a newspaper under your bedding?"

I nodded, but she didn't notice.

"Maybe I should change it," she said.

I agreed. I'd grown quite bored of the baseball updates. I watched her as she went to the day's paper, ripped it into long strips, section by section, and returned to my crate. I stayed at the back of the cage while she cleaned out all the old pellets that Nigel had put in there a week earlier. Then she placed all the shredded paper inside and nicely smoothed it out.

"I hope that's okay for now."

I twitched my nose. New reading material at last!

She shut the gate and went over to the kitchen and began preparing her own food. "It's an absolute shame about what happened to Nigel. I'm still in shock. He was such a good neighbor too."

I'd stopped listening, because a headline on one of the shreds of paper had caught my eye. I quickly circled my body around to read it.

LOCAL ANTIQUE STORE OWNER DEAD OF HEART ATTACK AT FAIR

I sat stock still, unsure of what to do next. No, that was not what happened. This wasn't a heart attack. I had *seen* someone running away from the tent just after he'd collapsed.

"If only we'd known that he'd been in poor health," she said.

No no no no. That was all wrong. I hopped up and down to get her attention. He had been murdered. I knew it.

Agnes looked down at me. "You're quite the excitable little animal. You know, I don't think Nigel ever told me your name."

Please not Fluffy. Please let it be something more adult.

She tilted her head. "You're white and pillowy and soft. I think I'll name you Marshmallow."

Oh God. I fell over on my back and stretched out my legs and played dead. That was nearly as bad as Fluffy.

"Well, Marshmallow, I'm going to bed. I'll see you first thing tomorrow, bright-eyed and bushy-tailed."

She waved goodnight at me. I remained stretched out on my back, unwilling to move.

When she was gone, I sat up. Grim thoughts filled my little skull. Chief among them was the fact that Nigel had been killed, and I was the only witness.

Chapter Six

AGNES

It was another quiet day in the library, and Agnes found her mind drifting as she crouched in the cooking section, reorganizing the books that people had misplaced when returning them to the shelves. Each book was numbered, and Esther got annoyed when they weren't in the correct order as it made them more difficult to find.

To Agnes' surprise, she had survived two nights with her new pet rabbit and was managing better than she'd expected. At least, she hadn't forgotten to feed Marshmallow, though she needed to make a note to buy something other than carrots. Wasn't that a curious thing? A bunny refusing carrots. But Marshmallow had made that very clear. Agnes hadn't expected an animal to be so good at communicating its needs, but this one was clever. She was half-convinced he understood what she was saying.

It occurred to Agnes that she had best make a note about picking up another type of vegetable. She might forget if she didn't write it down. She dropped the book she'd been holding onto the floor, the hardcover flipping open.

Agnes rummaged in her pocket and found a piece of

paper. Now, where was her pen? She always kept one on her, so she knew it had to be somewhere.

She patted her pockets again, becoming concerned. Then, she remembered where it was and almost laughed. *Agnes, you silly goose, it's in your hair!* She scolded herself the way her grandmother would have.

"What are you doing on the floor, Agnes?"

The harsh tone of Esther's voice surprised Agnes. Her boss could be strict, but she usually reserved that for the unruly children.

Agnes turned around, forgetting about her pen. Esther's arms were crossed, her thin lips pulled down in a tight frown. Agnes started to stutter out an explanation, but Esther didn't give her a chance.

"You're reading on the job again, aren't you? Honestly, Agnes, we haven't got time for you to behave like this. Put that book away and get up."

Instead of defending herself, Agnes jumped up, hurrying to obey Esther's orders. The fast movement caused her to stumble and she bumped into the shelf, knocking over a row of books.

Oh dear. Feeling guilty, Agnes turned to her boss.

Esther did not look impressed. Her eyes flashed in annoyance and she raised her hand to her forehead, rubbing it as though she'd gotten a headache all of a sudden. "You are a test of patience sometimes, Agnes. I do hope you're going to be in better form tomorrow night."

Agnes began trying to put the books upright again. She hated having Esther upset with her. "What's happening tomorrow night?"

"The Announcement Dinner, of course," Esther said, clearly annoyed that she had to state the obvious. "Just because they've had to change how they determine the Bake-Off competitors doesn't mean it's not happening."

Agnes supposed she should have known that. Every year, the festival committee organized a party at the community center. There, they announced the finalists for the Warrenton Bake-Off, plus some of the other smaller fair competitions. There was a large buffet and live music. It was very popular with the townspeople and visitors alike. Everyone went.

Which was exactly why Agnes hadn't been planning on attending. She'd gone a few times with her grandmother, but crowds weren't her thing. She would much prefer to be curled up at home with a cup of tea and a good book.

"I don't know if I can go to the dinner this year," Agnes said, trying to think of a lie that wouldn't lead to Esther bullying her into attending. "I'm taking care of Nigel's rabbit. I don't know if I should leave him alone at night."

"Don't be ridiculous, Agnes. Of course, you can leave it alone. Anyways, you must come to the dinner. I need you there to help me talk to donors."

Esther sighed and ran her hand over her forehead again. Did she look more stressed than she normally did when Agnes made a mistake? The lines around her lips seemed more pronounced, and there was a lot of gray visible in her roots.

"The library isn't doing well, Agnes," Esther admitted, her voice growing softer and less annoyed. "I'm hoping we can get some donations tomorrow or we might have to close. Josephine Charles is one of the judges this year. Goodness knows she's got money to donate since her husband died, and Dr. Michaels can be very generous. His wife isn't around to drag him, but I trust one of the other women will. And there's always the visitors. I have to do a bit more research on them, but I'm sure some would be willing to help, if we approach them right."

Agnes felt anxious listening to Esther. Her boss had mentioned the library lacking funds a few times, but she hadn't realized it was so bad. "Of course I'll come, Esther," Agnes assured her. "I didn't realize it was so important. What can I do to help?"

Esther smiled, then she scanned Agnes with a critical eye and sniffed. "Well, you might try dressing your age for a change, Agnes. You could be quite pretty if you tried a bit. Maybe let your hair down and don't wear so much gingham."

"Oh." Agnes wasn't certain what else to say. She was sure Esther hadn't meant to be mean. "I suppose I can try."

"Good," Esther said, rubbing her temples once more. She turned to leave, but just before, she gave Agnes a final look. "This is important, you understand? I'm counting on you. Don't let me down."

Chapter Seven

MURDER BUNNY

It was seven o'clock the next morning when I decided to become a sleuth.

This wasn't an easy decision. One doesn't suddenly commit oneself to the investigation of criminals and the pursuit of justice. Such a grand life decision shouldn't occur as suddenly as deciding to take a hot bath on a cold night. One must really take time to reflect, to consider one's calling. Nigel told me that he'd always consulted with his childhood minister before doing anything rash.

I didn't have a minister, so I spent the night alone peering deep within my little furry bunny soul. Sleep had been a distant dream, and soon I'd arrived at a terrible truth.

I couldn't very well allow Nigel's death to go unsolved.

I discovered that I'd somehow grown a conscience. It's a terrible thing to have happen to you, and I don't recommend it at all. One wouldn't know it from the way I treated Nigel while he was alive. I'd ignored him, run around him, avoided him, rejected his food, even slipped out of my cage for no reason at all. I was a bad bunny, but those were my younger, wilder days.

Now I was in my mature years, my fur thinning ever so slightly and my whiskers no longer twitching at the merest mention of a bagged vegetable medley. I'd calmed down immensely, and in a moment of uncharacteristic self-admiration, I might even admit that I'd grown wiser.

But as that first yellow beam of morning light struck my water bottle, I lifted my head. That's when I knew my course.

I had to solve this murder.

I possess several excellent attributes for a sleuth. I have strong powers of observation, analysis, and memory. And since I'm only noticed by most humans when I run around, this role is a natural fit for me.

I am not—repeat, *not*—a dumb bunny.

But I couldn't do it alone.

Even if I were to stack myself on top of four other bunnies inside a trench coat, I couldn't pass for a human. I don't have opposable thumbs or vocal cords or the ability to walk upright.

To solve Nigel's murder, I'd need someone who could drive, someone who could speak, someone who would be taken seriously. Someone with extra time on her hands. Someone with hands.

I heard the footsteps coming down the stairs. Into the kitchen walked Agnes, in her dowdy bathrobe and little ladybug slippers.

I needed someone like her.

———

Over the next half hour, as she prepared her morning oatmeal, I studied Agnes intently.

She was too young to be old but acted too old to be young. I'd never thought about Nigel's age because his personality was so strong that it didn't matter. But Agnes was a different sort, an odd duck, definitely pleasant but withdrawn in a way that made you tilt your head and wonder how someone could've ended up like that.

She sat at the kitchen table, placing her chopped walnuts and her dried fruit in a precise pinwheel design into her bowl. Then, using a spoon, she sprinkled brown sugar over the creation.

"Oh drat," she said.

I looked at her as intently as possible, twitching my nose. She noticed me.

"Marshmallow, I put half a spoon too much brown sugar and ruined my design," she said. "This is the absolute pits."

She pushed the bowl away and sipped her tea instead. If I were more attentive, I would've tried to hear what she started muttering to herself. But my mind was a thousand miles away, thinking about Nigel's murder.

The culprit had to be another baker. I was sure of that much. It had to be someone who was willing to go to extraordinary lengths to win the golden spoon trophy, even if that meant killing the competition. Nigel, as the five-year champion of the Warrenton Bake-Off, was the most obvious target. I knew that his competitors had stood in awe of him for years. There were plenty of them that would have wanted to get their hands on his new carrot cake recipe. But which one would have been willing to kill for it?

I knew the first step for a detective was to investigate the suspects. The problem was that I didn't know where baking people would congregate or how I would get to them.

The telephone rang, and Agnes ran to pick it up. As she lifted it from the cradle, it slipped out of her fingers and hit the floor.

"Oh no," she squeaked, as she crouched to the floor to pick it up. "Hello? Oh hi Cindy." She was looking at me distantly, not at me but through me. Her hair had fallen into her eyes and her mouth hung slightly open. She hadn't put any makeup on and her face looked pale and drawn and confused.

"No, I'm not working today," she said. "Yeah, you can come over, I don't see why not. Oh I know--it was just terrible about Nigel. Sure, bring the kids. We'll make cookies. Of course I'll be here, just come by whenever. You know I never go anywhere. Okay, bye."

She replaced the phone in the cradle and slid down the wall until she was fully sitting on the floor. Her eyes found mine.

"I'm sorry, Marshmallow. This is going to be a hard day for you." She sighed. "I'd better check that I have all the ingredients. If not, I'll need to go to the specialty market."

My ears perked up at that one. The speciality market was the place where bakers congregated.

She rose to her feet and went through the pantry, one by one setting onto the counter a series of small bottles of flavorings and spices, a bag of sugar, and a ceramic jar of flour. "Okay, never mind. I think Grandma left us all set."

Her back was turned to me. This was my opportunity to set in motion the wheels of justice. Agnes wouldn't know why I was acting like a crazed maniac but that was no concern of mine. I needed to find out who killed Nigel.

I kicked open my door, bolted out, took three long steps, then leapt onto the countertop.

"Marshmallow!" she shouted.

I ignored her and streaked along the counter, wreaking havoc. I slid into the row of bottled spices and flavorings. They scattered like a set of bowling pins.

As she was trying to right them, I quickly gnawed a hole in the bag of sugar. A small river of granules began trickling onto the floor.

"My goodness, what is wrong with you!?" she said.

Agnes lunged for me, but I sidestepped her. She slipped on the sugar and went down, all the way to the linoleum. That was a shame, but I needed to complete the savage destruction with a final *coup de grace*.

Using my nose, I nudged the ceramic jar of flour to the edge of the counter.

Agnes looked up from the floor and a look of horror crossed her face. "No, Marshmallow, don't—"

I gave it a final nudge. The ceramic jar pitched over and fell in slow-motion to the floor. I watched it crack in half. I watched the refined white flour plume up in a horrible mushroom cloud.

The baking catastrophe was reflected in my eyes.

Agnes lowered her head to the floor. Her face and hair and chest were totally covered in white flour.

"Now I'm going to have to go to Margie's," she said.

That was the opportunity. I dashed off the counter, ran to her keys, picked them up in my mouth, and hopped to the door. There I turned and faced her, waiting.

Agnes stared at me, flummoxed and flabbergasted.

"Do you want to come with me, Marshmallow?"

I wagged my tail extra fast. *Yes I do.* She groaned and pulled herself to her feet. "Well all right then. I'm going to have to change first." Her eyes fell upon me and there was sadness in them. "I don't know what I'm going to do with you. That flour jar was the one my grandma had picked out. She loved it. I'm going to have to get a new one now."

I knew I'd acted like an absolute prat, but she would forgive me, someday.

Chapter Eight

MURDER BUNNY

Margie's Batter Chatter was an institution in Warrenton.

Housed in a historic octagonal red barn, it had been opened by Margaret McQuilly nearly half a century ago. Better known as Margie, she still ruled the store with a keen eye for what amateur and professional bakers alike might need. Whatever a person wanted, she could get there, baking-wise, from amaranth flour to beet sugar to dried dandelions to plastic baby toppers.

The other thing a person could find there was gossip. Margie knew that, of course, and it was one of the main draws in the community. I'd visited plenty of times, because Nigel had loved to carry me around in public. Oh, I won't mince words: He'd been an absolute attention hog, and I was the vehicle that brought it to him.

Agnes didn't know this, of course. Which is why she nearly dropped my carrier in shock as she walked into the Batter Chatter and was greeted with a shout.

"Fluffy!"

Three women were facing us. Margie behind the till, her eldest granddaughter Ashley stocking a shelf, and a middle-aged shopper wearing a cloche hat and a bad attitude on the far side of the store. I'd seen her before and remembered her name: Sandra Swat.

"You know him?" said Agnes.

"Of course we do," said Margie. "Fluffy is our favorite!"

I braced myself for the onslaught. It arrived within seconds, with all three women encircling my carrier and lifting me up and cooing at me. I'm no celebrity, but one must keep one's fans satisfied, so I obliged by sniffing their fingers, twitching my ears, and running in a couple of excited circles when they eventually returned me to my crate.

They placed me on a barrel in the corner so that Agnes could begin shopping. It was the best seat for my purposes, giving me a clear view of the store and letting me hear the conversation.

"You must tell us how on earth you came to possess Fluffy," said Margie, returning to the cash register. "Everybody was wondering what had happened to him."

"I don't know," she admitted. "He just sort of... leaped out of his cage and sat on my foot."

Ashley was stacking boxes of cornmeal. "That bunny is the cutest thing I've ever seen."

"I believe God created him to be the most adorable creature ever," added Sandra.

I shut my eyes and ears. These women were going to give me an inflated sense of myself. That wouldn't do. I always dislike it when people tell me things I already know.

"Poor Nigel," said Margie. "We lost an excellent baker."

Sandra lifted her nose into the air. "I never liked that man, and now he's pooched the entire competition on his way out."

"What's happening with the Bake-Off?" said Agnes. "I've been too distracted with the death and the bunny to follow."

"It's still happening," replied Margie, "but the judges are picking the competitors in a different way this year."

"How?" said Agnes. She was already picking items off the shelf and placing them in her basket.

Margie went back to the business side of the counter. "That is shrouded in mystery. They say that they will reveal everything by tomorrow evening."

"They'd better," said Sandra. "I'll only have five days to prepare."

Ashley looked up at her. "You sound pretty sure that you'll be one of the finalists."

I liked her. Ashley was a cool customer already, at the age of sixteen.

"Indeed I am, young lady. I've been a finalist for the past three years. This time, I intend to win. Finally."

That last word held a dark meaning. There was a lot of significance sitting behind it.

My nose twitched in disgust. I decided I really didn't like her. Sandra Lee had always held herself as though she were royalty that had descended upon this small town to bless its specialty baking store with her inestimable presence. And while she had never struck me as a decent person before, it was even less so now. I wouldn't trust her with a bag of spinach. She needed to be brought down a peg, but just how I was going to accomplish that, I didn't know.

"What about you, Agnes?" said Margie, glancing at her shopping cart. "Are you preparing for a possible selection?"

"No," my new owner muttered, "I couldn't ever think of competing."

"Then why all the ingredients, dear? I would assume you're prepping for the big weekend."

Agnes looked down at her shopping basket as if for the first time. "This is just for fun. A friend is coming over with her children. We're going to make cookies."

"Isn't that nice," said Sandra. I could almost smell the condescension.

Agnes smiled at her, but her body language showed her extreme discomfort. "Margie, can I ask where the quick oats are?"

"Over on the shelf nearest the door."

Sandra cleared her throat. "But if they're for cookies, you'd best purchase the whole rolled oats. It guarantees a chewier texture."

"Thank you," said Agnes.

"You're welcome."

Agnes turned away, looking distinctly chastised. I didn't like the way that Sandra was speaking to her.

The door swung open and a thin man dressed in a natty gray suit sauntered into the historic barn-turned-shop. His thin face wore a look of disdain and his black beady eyes shifted left and right as though controlled by invisible strings. His lips were pursed together tightly.

"Good morning, Sebastian," said Margie with a little too much politeness in her voice.

"Of course it's a good morning," he replied. "I'm one day closer to winning the Bake-Off."

"You say that every year," said Sandra, her back turned, pretending to inspect a bottle of almond extract.

"It's going to happen," he said, "this year, finally. Now that Nigel's out of the picture. Has anybody seen his famous carrot cake recipe that was supposed to win all the prizes?" His fingers made air quotes around the words *famous carrot cake recipe*.

"No," said Margie, "and I doubt we ever will."

"I'd certainly like to get my hands on it," he said.

"As would I," added Sandra.

You know what they say about rabbit blood: it's just like human blood. And mine was starting to boil. I didn't like how they were so cavalierly dismissing the life of a good man who never hurt anybody and lived to make amazing desserts that he sometimes let me taste.

Sebastian caught sight of me in my carrier, and his lip sneered. "Whose animal is this?"

"It was Nigel's," said Margie, "and now it's hers."

Agnes gave him a wan smile, tried to place a box of oats into her basket, but it slipped and fell onto the floor.

"Hopeless," he muttered under his breath. Then he turned back to me and peered at my neck. "Hello now, what's this?"

"What's what?" said Margie.

"The item on the bunny's collar."

For a moment, I froze. I'd honestly forgotten that I was wearing a collar. Nigel had placed it on me a few weeks earlier with no explanation, no self-narration. To be honest, I didn't even notice it was there.

Margie came over, as did Ashley, Agnes, and even Sandra. Five humans all peering at me. My eyes flicked around the group.

"I don't know," said Margie.

"It looks like a bell," said Ashley.

"It looks expensive," added Sandra. "Nigel always liked to overspoil that creature."

"Let me take a better look," Sebastian said. He unlocked my carrier and reached towards me. I growled.

"You'd better back down," said Ashley.

"I'm not going to hurt him."

"That's not who we're worried about," said Margie.

His hands grabbed my fur. I couldn't tolerate this creep touching me. So I bit him on the hand. I bit *hard*. Almost enough to draw blood.

Sebastian yelped and leapt back, yanking his hand out of my carrier. Agnes meekly closed the carrier door and locked it. "I'm sorry, that was uncalled for," she said diplomatically. "He's had a hard week, what with a new owner and new home and everything."

"That thing should be put down," he spat, rubbing his hand.

Margie steered him away from me. "There there, let's take you in the back and get your hand cleaned up."

Sebastian had begun whining. "Who brings a wild animal like that into a store? It doesn't even make sense to keep it alive."

"I know, I know," said Margie, arm across her customer's shoulders.

Agnes looked mortified. I sat there, smug in my knowledge that Sebastian was a horrible human being who deserved everything I gave him, and more.

I watched as Ashley rang up Agnes at the till. Agnes asked the young girl about ordering another ceramic jar. I guess she was more attached to the one I broke than I realized. I felt a bit guilty about that, but it seemed like it could be replaced quite easily. Margie's Batter Chatter was getting a shipment tomorrow.

A few minutes later, we were back in the car, heading home.

And I was thinking about the two new suspects.

Chapter Nine

MURDER BUNNY

Later that morning, Cindy and her brood swept into Agnes' home like a gang of flying winged monkeys.

There were three shrieking children, all girls, but I didn't catch any of their names. I didn't want to. I was in my cage, and the banshees instantly set upon me with rabid ferocity, dropping things on my back, trying to poke me with fingers and silverware. I burrowed under my litter, shivering in fear.

"Look he's hiding!" one shouted.

Yes, I was hiding. I'm a strong bunny but there's only so much I can do to defend myself against packs of small predatory humans who haven't been socialized yet. They began shaking the cage. My ears were flat against my neck now. It felt like the world was ending.

Finally the racket grew so unbearable that Agnes stepped in.

"Girls, leave Marshmallow alone," she said. "He's had a very difficult week."

"But we want to play with him!" shouted one.

Cindy grew stern. "Listen to Auntie Agnes, children."

"Oh gosh," Agnes said, looking at her friend. "I've told you I don't like when they call me Auntie. I'm not their aunt."

"It's just an expression, Aggie," Cindy reassured her.

Then, to my surprise, Agnes popped open the door and released me from the cage.

"Come out, Marshmallow," she said, "the children want to meet you."

I squeaked in horror. The children screamed in delight. That made me squeak again; they screamed again. Then I squeaked a third time, which distracted them enough for me to race out of the cage, between their legs, and out of the kitchen.

I thumped through the house, *pat a pat a pat a pat*, hearing the small thunder of six legs behind me. I streaked behind the sofa, which was a heavy Victorian disaster with rump dents in its faded floral fabric. It had been shoved almost up against the back of the living room wall, with one end blocked by an old grandfather clock and the other wedged into the corner. There was just enough room for me to squiggle behind it.

I'd wedged myself into the tightest space possible, protected from all the grubby little hands. And that's where I stayed and waited out the attack. The demons leaped on the cushions, ran broomsticks around underneath, tried in vain to drag the couch away from the sofa. Nothing worked.

I was safe.

At last Cindy's children lost interest in me and scattered. I heard them run upstairs, and when the last set of footsteps had thundered up the staircase, I breathed a small sigh of relief. Let me tell you, a bunny's life isn't always a piece of cake. Danger lurks outside every cage. Out there, in the wild, you never know when the silent swoop from an aerial predator means the end.

Still, at least children don't want to kill you, at least not on purpose. And you humans may be clever but your kind is quite slow. I've never known any rabbit who couldn't outstrip a human. We dash faster than some of you drive.

I wriggled out from behind the couch and hotfooted it over to the kitchen. I stood at the edge of the doorway and peered around the doorjamb. Cindy and Agnes were standing at the counter, their hands deep in the bowls, the baking sheets already prewarming in the oven.

"That bunny is so cute," said Cindy. "My kids would love him as a pet."

"I'm growing fond of him actually," said Agnes.

"Guess that means you're not interested in giving him up?"

"He's got quite a little personality. I mean, he leapt onto this counter this morning and broke everything. I had to take him to Margie's to buy everything new because he wouldn't give up the keys!"

"That's a little strange," said Cindy.

"What is?"

"Taking your rabbit out to a store."

"I didn't have a choice! He has a mind of his own."

"So it would seem. Be careful that you don't get too attached to him. He's not a human."

Agnes sighed, rolled her eyes. I wanted to tell her not to worry too much about it. Most people feel instantly attached to me. It's the bunny's curse.

"Anyways, what are you feeding him?"

"I tried carrots but he won't eat them."

"Do you know what Nigel fed him?"

"No."

Too late I thought of how, that morning, I could've written *watercress* in the sugar on the floor. *Le esprit d'escalier*. Sigh.

Cindy peered out the window. "Wasn't that Nigel's house

right over there? Down the block. You could snoop around inside and find out."

Agnes grew red-faced. "I don't think that would be a good idea, Cindy. It would be illegal."

"Well, not everything illegal is wrong. Did you know that it's still illegal to eat snakes on Sunday in Kansas?"

"You would eat snakes *any* day?"

Cindy looked at her. "No, but shouldn't it be an option for those weirdos who enjoy the taste of reptiles? Why should they have to wait for Monday? There's nothing like a good Sunday dinner of broiled boa constrictor."

Agnes held an embarrassed hand up to her mouth. "You are absolutely too much, Cindy."

"Don't I know it." Cindy pulled a sheet from the oven, wetted her hands in the sink, and began forming balls of dough. "Oh wait. I forgot they wanted to do this." Cindy cupped her hands around her mouth and shouted. "Kids! We need help!"

I squeaked. This wouldn't do, at all. I dashed under the kitchen table and prayed that my tiny torturers wouldn't see me there.

The three girls arrived in a stampede of shoes. The oldest one, maybe thirteen, looked at Agnes and the ingredients. "Are you making oatmeal raisin cookies?"

"Yes," said Agnes tentatively.

The girl stood next to her, inspecting the array of bottles and bags. "Did you add the salt?"

Agnes blanched. A nervous hand fluttered up to the base of her throat. "Um, no I did not. That was unfortunately forgotten."

The girl swiped a finger in the bowl and tasted the dough. "I think you used cold butter. It should be room temperature."

"That's enough, Fran," said Cindy to her daughter.

But Fran wasn't done yet. She looked at the cookie sheet. "The sheet is dark, Mom. You can't bake cookies on unlined dark cookie sheets. They have to be light and lined with parchment paper."

"Well, this is the way we're doing it," said Cindy. "Nobody here has aspirations of professionalism."

Agnes looked pained.

"Maybe *you* don't..." Fran began.

"Sweetie, why don't you and your sisters go play with the bunny again."

"We can't find him!" the littlest one shouted.

Cindy's phone rang. She picked up and listened for a moment. "Yes, of course. I'll take the girls and go now."

She disconnected. "It's Scott. He says the chimney contractor called him and they need me to come home right away. There's something wrong with the flue."

Agnes deflated. I felt sorry for her. She'd suffered so much this morning to make this baking afternoon possible.

"Okay," she said.

"Raincheck?" Cindy glanced at the dough. "Maybe next time we can try a different recipe."

"Okay," Agnes said again.

Cindy hugged her friend and gathered her things. "All right kids, let's go. Mommy's needed at home."

"But we didn't get the cookies yet!" shouted the middle one.

"I'm sure Aunt Agnes will save you some for next time."

Agnes lowered her chin to her chest and muttered, "I'm not their aunt."

"It's just an expression, Agnes." She corralled the three girls and pushed them out the door. "Let's talk soon, sweetheart."

She kissed Agnes' cheek, and the door closed, and then it was just the two of us.

I cautiously crawled out from beneath the table. Agnes saw me and softened. "There you are."

I lifted my two front paws into the air to show her that I'd understood her. And that I appreciated her. After all, she was feeding me.

She trudged back to the counter and reluctantly formed the dough into balls, placed them on the baking sheet, and slid it into the oven. Then she collapsed at the kitchen table.

"I don't think I have a future as a baker," she said. "I really don't."

I curled up on her left foot. She smiled down at me. We must've both fallen asleep, because the next thing I knew, she was pushing me off.

"My goodness, the cookies!" she shouted.

The black smoke practically billowed out of the oven when she opened it. The cookies looked like chunks of crusted volcanic rock.

Agnes quickly yanked up the window to get some air in the place. "Maybe next time it will be better."

Chapter Ten

AGNES

Later that evening, Agnes stood before the long mirror in her grandmother's old room. It still had all her grandmother's old things, including the queen bed with the pink floral bedspread, a dressing table with a large jewelry box, and the white armoire full of her clothes. At some point, Agnes would have to clear out the room, but she couldn't bear to do it just yet. Besides, she found it useful having her grandmother's old things around.

Dolores Brooms had been a very fashionable woman. She had tons of beautiful clothes and fancy jewelry. Agnes didn't often have occasions to use the jewelry, but most of the dresses fit her. She'd been enjoying choosing different ones to wear and mix with her own wardrobe.

The problem was that Esther didn't seem to like Dolores' outfits. Before her grandmother's death, Agnes had heard her boss compliment her grandmother plenty of times, but it seemed that the head librarian was more particular about what Agnes wore.

Agnes spun around in the pink suit she'd found. It had a neat pencil skirt that was only a little big on her, and the jacket was snug, accentuating her shoulders. Did it look old?

It wasn't something Agnes would typically have worn, so maybe Esther would like that. Plus, something about the suit screamed businesswoman. That should be helpful if they were trying to get people to donate.

The idea of talking to everyone tonight and trying to convince them to give the library money made Agnes' chest flutter with anxiety. She already felt uncomfortable at social events with more than a handful of people. Now, Esther expected her to be charming and win people over.

A whistled tune came through the open window. Agnes stopped looking at her reflection and turned toward the noise. It was a song her grandmother had loved to sing, and it almost sounded like it was coming from her backyard.

Not certain what she was expecting to see, Agnes hurried over to the window. She looked outside and her curiosity dissipated into annoyance. It was her Uncle Curtis.

For some reason, he'd taken off his shirt and was dressed only in a pair of old denim shorts. His large stomach protruded over the edge. From her high vantage point, Agnes could see the bald patch on the top of his head, which he usually tried to hide with a comb over. However, the wind had blown the strands of dark hair over to the side.

He stood over the barbecue, whistling happily to himself. Smoke wafted up towards Agnes and she could smell that he had burgers cooking.

"Uncle Curtis, what are you doing?" Agnes called down to him.

He looked up at her and waved, as though it were a completely normal thing for him to be barbecuing on some-one's property without their permission. "Oh hey, Aggie. I'd offer you some, but I'm afraid I only got three patties left."

That seemed like it should have been enough to share, but

that wasn't relevant just now. "I meant, why are you cooking dinner in my backyard?"

"Well, I would've come inside, but you've got the deadbolt locked. That's silly, Aggie. What if there was a fire? How could the firemen get inside to save you?"

"Why would there be a fire?"

"I don't know. Maybe you were thinking of trying cooking again." Uncle Curtis laughed loudly at his own joke.

Agnes crossed her arms. He was referring to the unfortunate incident when she, age twelve, had tried to make dinner as a surprise for her grandmother. It hadn't gone well. Dolores had used her fire extinguisher and put everything out. There had been no need to get the firemen involved.

Pointing that out seemed like a bad comeback, however.

"What the hell are you wearing?" he said, staring up at Agnes as though seeing her properly for the first time. "Are you running a board meeting from fifteen years ago?"

"What?" Agnes didn't understand his comment.

"I'm saying, you're dressed like my mom. Actually, she had a suit that looked just like that."

Feeling embarrassed and uncertain what to say, Agnes lied. "No, I'm just getting ready for the dinner tonight. I have to network while I'm there."

Uncle Curtis laughed again. "You'll stand out. I hope you like being the center of attention!"

Agnes huffed and closed the window. There was no use yelling at her uncle. He wouldn't leave anyway, and at least this time he hadn't been able to get inside. Hopefully he'd be gone before she had to leave.

She considered the business suit one last time in the mirror before taking it off. Maybe Uncle Curtis was right. She surveyed the other outfits she'd laid out on the bed and lifted up a long pink dress. It had a high collar, and there was something Elizabethan about the puffy sleeves.

Agnes put it on and then spent the next hour styling herself. It was longer than she normally took, but she felt anxious and she did want to please Esther.

By the time she was finished, however, she was quite satisfied. She felt regal, in the long pink dress with her hair in a graceful bun and her grandmother's pink pearls in her ears. This was much nicer than the business suit, she decided. After all, people liked to dress fancy when they went to fundraising events.

Feeling pleased with herself, Agnes descended the stairs. To her surprise, Marshmallow was sitting at the bottom. He'd gotten out of his carrier again. Agnes made a note to remind herself to get that lock fixed.

He hopped up and down and wiggled his ears at her in excitement.

"Do you think I look pretty, Marshmallow?" Agnes asked, twirling for him when she reached the bottom of the steps.

He continued hopping, which she took as a yes. He was quite the excitable creature. Agnes decided to leave him out of his crate while she went out. He didn't seem to like being cooped up and, besides the incident with her baking supplies, he never made a mess.

Agnes went to the door and realized the bunny was following her.

She paused and turned to him. "No, you can't come with me. Not this time."

The bunny stopped bouncing. His ears drooped down to the sides. He turned away and retreated under the table.

Agnes watched in amazement. "I swear you understand me."

It was an absolute marvel, but Agnes didn't have time to stop and think about Marshmallow. She checked the clock on the kitchen wall. Oh no! She was already running late.

"Wish me luck, Marshmallow!" Agnes called, and then hurried out the house.

Chapter Eleven

AGNES

Agnes arrived at the town hall about fifteen minutes after Esther had told her to be there. She grabbed her black purse and raced from her car across the parking lot to the entrance. It was difficult to run in kitten heels and the long pink dress, but she managed to make it without falling on her face, which was a small victory for Agnes.

The entrance had been decorated with fairy lights, white ribbons and metallic balloons. The sounds of the seventies hits that the DJ played mingled with the chatter of the crowd, reverberating in Agnes' ears. It grew louder as she approached, and her nerves increased with the noise.

There were so many people. She grew anxious.

A doorman waited at the entrance to check Agnes' ticket. He was a large middle-aged man with broad shoulders. She pulled out the stub that her boss had given her. He held it for a while though he barely glanced at it. Instead, he ran his eyes over Agnes' outfit. He let out a strange chuckle, but passed it back and let her in without saying a word.

Inside, the hall had been arranged for a party. There was a cocktail bar and buffet table to the far left. A series of tables

and chairs filled that half of the room before they disappeared, making room for a large dance floor in front of the
stage where a DJ was controlling the music. At some point,
Mrs. Harrison, who organized the festival each year, would
get up to announce the finalists in the various competitions.

Most people clustered around the buffet, grabbing dinner
before they began dancing. That suited Agnes fine. She felt
much more comfortable eating than she did dancing. She had
two left feet.

Before she'd made it to the buffet line, she felt a hand on
her shoulder. "There you are, Agnes," said a voice.

It was Esther. She wore a floor-length black dress, with a
modest neckline and no sleeves, revealing her thin, wrinkled
arms. She'd swapped her typical bun for a long braid that
draped over her shoulder.

Esther grabbed Agnes by the elbow and spun her all the
way around so that she could see her. The head librarian
frowned. "What are you wearing? Didn't I tell you to dress
your age? Goodness, child, you're more covered than I am.
What are these sleeves?"

Agnes blushed, feeling embarrassed as her boss pinched
the puffy sleeves on the dress, staring at them with a disapproving frown. She should have worn the dress suit after all.
Why had she listened to her uncle? He didn't know anything
about fashion.

"Honestly, it's no wonder you're single, Agnes," Esther
said. She reached over and untied the lace around the neck of
the dress, trying to pull it open so that it revealed Agnes'
neck. It didn't seem to open as much as Esther would have
liked, because she gave an annoyed huff before spinning
Agnes around once more and trying to fix her hair. She pulled
out all the golden pins, destroying the bun that Agnes had
agonized over: she'd wanted it to be perfect for tonight,
trying to ensure that she didn't have stray hairs out of place

like usual. She'd felt certain Esther, of all people, would have approved of a bun, but it seemed she'd bungled even that.

Once Agnes' hair was loose around her neck, her boss considered her again. Esther tutted a few times and then sighed. "It'll have to do. Now, come on. There's someone I've been wanting you to meet."

Esther took Agnes' elbow and pulled her into the crowd towards a tall, older man who was dressed in a fine gray suit. He had a short, neatly-groomed brown goatee, with flecks of silver near the corners of the mustache. His dark hair was slicked back on his head, highlighting high cheekbones and a strong jaw. From a distance, he looked about Agnes' own age, but as she drew closer, she could see lines around his eyes and on his forehead, and she guessed he was somewhere in his fifties.

"Agnes, this is Tobias Thornton. He's one of the most successful antique dealers in the state. Aren't we lucky to have him visiting Warrenton?" She nudged Agnes, who realized that was her cue to nod. Then, turning back to Tobias, Esther continued. "This is another library employee, Agnes Brooms. She's such a dear, and she lives right next to the antique store we have here. I think you two will really hit it off."

"A pleasure, Ms. Brooms." Tobias reached out and took Agnes' hand. He brought it to his lips and kissed it. There was a large gold ring with a bright red stone on his finger. Agnes noticed it as it brushed against her fingers. "Do you have much interest in antiques?"

Feeling out of her element, Agnes pulled her hand away from his grip. She wasn't certain if he was trying to flirt with her or just being polite. What had Esther told this man, and what did she expect Agnes to say?

Esther nudged Agnes, prompting her to respond.

"Not really," Agnes squeaked. Then, seeing her boss

gesturing for her to continue, she kept talking, letting the words escape from her mouth. "I live next door to Nigel. Lived... I mean, I'm still alive. But Nigel isn't. He died. At the fair. But you probably know that, everyone's been talking about it. It was tragic. Anyway, he was the one who owned the antique store. I didn't go in much—but, I mean, I've adopted his pet bunny now. That's been interesting. Did you know rabbits don't like carrots?"

Agnes finally clamped her mouth shut. She shouldn't have said any of that. That wouldn't help them get funds for the library at all.

Beside her, Esther groaned and covered her eyes with her hand. Tobias tilted his head to the side, looking at Agnes quizzically.

"I don't know much about rabbits." The older man smiled politely at Agnes. "But I did hear about your neighbor. Heart attack, wasn't it? Quite unfortunate. I rather think his carrot cake would have won."

"Oh yes," Esther agreed, speaking before Agnes had a chance. "Nigel was a divine baker. You're one of the judges this year, aren't you, Tobias? You must like baking, correct?"

"Indeed."

"Agnes' grandmother was an excellent baker. She knows all about it."

"Oh yes," Agnes agreed, guessing that this was the correct answer. She saw Esther nod approvingly, so she continued. "But she's dead now."

"That's too bad," he said.

Esther shook her head. Agnes had gone in the wrong direction. She tried to correct course.

"But I baked some cookies earlier today. Although that was a bit of a disaster. And Marshmallow destroyed all the ingredients so that I'd be forced to take him to the store, which I did, and then I had twice as much to clean."

Tobias' eyebrows pulled together and his wrinkles became more pronounced as he looked at Agnes, confused by her once more. "I'm sorry, who's Marshmallow?"

"The rabbit," Agnes explained. "That's his name. I mean, actually I think his name is Fluffy. Only I didn't know that when I adopted him, so I named him Marshmallow. You know, I'm not sure if he really cares. He's very clever though. I caught him studying a crossword puzzle yesterday. Have you ever seen a bunny do a crossword puzzle?"

"Can't say that I have."

Esther elbowed Agnes a bit more sharply this time. Agnes looked at her, and Esther turned her head so that she was briefly hidden from Tobias.

Focus on the library, she mouthed.

Of course. Agnes felt guilty. She ought to be concentrating on her main mission for the evening. She turned back to the antique dealer. "So, Mr. Thornton, you must do quite well for yourself. Would you be interested in making a donation to the town library? We're running low on funds."

Esther groaned in exasperation.

Tobias coughed uncomfortably. "You may have misunderstood my status. Antiquing isn't quite as lucrative a business as you think, young lady. Would you both excuse me?"

"Of course," said Esther. "I'll find you in a few minutes, after I track down Esmerelda. You're going to love chatting with her!"

Her forced smile was strong enough to crack walnuts. Tobias returned a polite nod, turned his back, and disappeared into the crowd.

Once they were alone, Esther turned to Agnes. The older woman did not look impressed. Her hands were on her hips, her lips were pulled into a tight frown, and she was shooting Agnes her strict over-the-glasses librarian glare.

"That is not how you get donations, Agnes," she hissed.

"You can't just ask for them like that. And why were you talking so much about Nigel's stupid animal? Goodness, you have no sense of how to communicate with people. I don't know why I thought you'd be helpful."

"I'm sorry--"

" Just get yourself some food and stay quiet. I'll try to smooth things over with Tobias, but I suspect the poor man will spend the rest of the night hiding from us. And I haven't seen Sebastian anywhere either. I wanted to talk to him as well."

"Again, please let me apologize, I just--"

Esther held up an annoyed hand. "Go stand over there and don't talk to anybody."

Feeling thoroughly chastised and embarrassed, Agnes lowered her head and went to the buffet table, following Esther's instructions. She should have known tonight would be a disaster. Now, she just had to hope that she could leave without making more of a fool of herself than she already had.

Chapter Twelve

AGNES

Agnes sat at a round table in the corner of the hall, hunched over a plate of pasta, pushing the food around mournfully with her fork. She was hoping not to be noticed. She was also feeling resentful that Esther had insisted that she come to the dinner in the first place. Didn't she know that socializing wasn't Agnes' strength? What had Esther expected would happen?

Suddenly, there was a thud as someone dropped onto the chair beside her. It was Dr. Michaels. The handsome widower was dressed in an old-fashioned plaid suit. Though he was past forty, his skin was smooth and the way he parted his blond hair in the center gave him a boyish look. He glanced at Agnes with the soft gray eyes that made the women of the town catch colds at least twice a week so that they had an excuse to visit his office.

"Hide me," he said, bending low and ducking behind a startled Agnes.

"Oh, sure," Agnes agreed, not certain if she should look at the doctor or her plate. "Who are you hiding from?"

"All of them," Dr. Michaels explained, peeping his head up

and glancing around Agnes to see if he'd been spotted. "Here, if you twist just like this, then I'll be mostly hidden."

He rested his hands on Agnes' chair, dangerously close to her legs. Agnes felt her heart stop for a moment in bewildered excitement. However, he was only pulling the chair to help hide him from most direct lines of vision.

Once he had Agnes in position, Dr. Michaels relaxed. He breathed a sigh of relief. "It's good to see you, Agnes. I don't think our paths have crossed since Dolores passed. What have you been up to?"

The handsome doctor smiled at Agnes. It was a smile that would make any woman swoon, and Agnes stumbled to find an answer that would impress him. She'd best not mention Marshmallow though. Esther had made it clear that Agnes talked about the bunny too much. She could tell him about the cookies she'd baked with Cindy, but then she'd have to admit that she'd burned them.

"I ordered a new ceramic container for my flour today. My old one broke."

"Ah. How... exciting." Dr. Michaels nodded and looked away. His tone made it evident that he found Agnes' story to be anything but.

But Agnes stayed committed to the story. "It was one that my grandmother had ordered special from Margie's. It had yellow daisies on it. Those were her favorite. They're my favorite too. They're so bright and cheerful and I thought it was funny to have flowers on the flour. Do you get it? Because they sound the same but one has petals and the other is used in baking. It's cute. Do you have a favorite flower?"

"I'm partial to the classic all-purpose," Dr. Michaels said, giving Agnes an amused smile.

"I don't think I've heard of an all-purpose flower before. What does it look like?" Then Agnes realized that he'd been joking. She covered her face with her hands, feeling mortified that she hadn't picked up on it sooner. "You're talking about baking flour, aren't you?"

Dr. Michaels chuckled. "You know, you're a real life-saver, Agnes. I haven't been able to sit down and have a moment of peace since I arrived."

"Is Esther harassing you for money?" Agnes asked, recalling that her boss had mentioned the doctor as a possible donor.

"The librarian? No, she's a bit old." He paused and raised an eyebrow, as though he'd just registered what Agnes asked. "Oh, you said *for money*?"

"The library needs money or it's going to be closed down," Agnes explained. "Esther is looking for donations. I'm supposed to be helping, but I'm not much good at it, I'm afraid. My outfit isn't the right one for the occasion, I said all the wrong things to the antique dealer, and now I've gone and told you that we're desperate for money as well. Esther is going to demote me to custodian."

Agnes had the epiphany as she spoke, and at the end she buried her face in her hands once more, wishing she didn't sound so whiny when speaking to the handsome doctor.

"Your dress is pretty," Dr. Michaels said, patting her shoulder. "It's very feminine. In fact, I think pink suits you."

Agnes wasn't certain if the doctor was teasing her or trying to console her, but she doubted that was true given the other reactions she'd gotten. Still, she looked up and smiled in gratitude. "I thought it seemed vintage," she admitted.

Dr. Michael was no longer looking at Agnes, however. His eyes had widened as he stared across the room. "Oh no. I've been spotted."

Without any farewell, the doctor rose to his feet and dashed away, leaving a bewildered Agnes. What had she said to scare him off this time?

It wasn't Agnes, however, as soon became clear to her, but Lilah Dorchester.

———

The middle-aged nurse was spilling out of a long blue dress with silver embroidery along the low neckline. She'd styled her short blond hair in a bob that curled around her neck, in a style that reminded Agnes of a nineteen-fifties housewife.

Lilah barreled through the crowd and up to Agnes' table. She slammed her hands down. "Did my eyes deceive me or were you just talking to Dr. Michaels?"

Despite Lilah's round face and bright pink lipstick, she still managed to be intimidating, and her voice was deep and husky and impossible to ignore.

Agnes squeaked. This must have been who Dr. Michaels was hiding from.

"I don't really know what I was doing," she said.

"I see two possibilities. You were trying to butter him up for the Bake-Off or you were throwing yourself at him like the rest of the single women in town. Which is it?"

"Neither." Agnes shook her head quickly. She hoped that would satisfy Lilah and that the woman would go in search of someone else to speak with. Agnes had finished eating, and the nurse's arrival had reminded her how desperately ready she was to leave.

"I'll trust it was the latter." Lilah snorted and, to Agnes' distress, sat down beside her. "Goodness knows the women here in Warrenton have gone mad for Dr. Michaels since he arrived. I don't know whose ridiculous idea it was to have him as one of the judges for the Bake-Off. I doubt he's ever so much as seen a mixer. Still, he's the only local on the panel. I wish he'd stay still so I could talk to him about the finalists."

"Oh, have they announced the finalists then?" Agnes

asked, trying to make conversation so as not to seem rude. It was a silly question though since she knew that they hadn't. None of the contestants for the fair's competitions had been announced yet.

"Apparently, they're not announcing them tonight," Lilah said, sounding distressed. "They're going to post a notice later on. Cutting it very close, I'd say. But that's not even the worst of it. They still haven't told us how they're going to decide since they canceled the preliminaries."

"Terrible."

"Nigel always was inconsiderate. I'm sure he timed his death just to throw all of us off." The nurse leaned forward and took one of the biscuits off Agnes' plate. She snapped a piece off and began chewing it loudly. "You don't happen to know what they did with his carrot cake when they found him, do you? I'd love to try a slice. The stingy old fart only gave me one bite, but I'm certain I tasted cardamom in there. I'd love to see if I couldn't piece his amazing recipe together."

She rolled her eyes on the word amazing, making it clear that she was exaggerating based on Nigel's own high opinion of himself.

"I don't know what happened to the cake. Maybe the police ate it?"

"How silly," said Lilah.

Agnes glanced towards the exit. "I'm afraid I have to be going now, Lilah. Good luck getting into the finals."

However, before Agnes could leave, she was interrupted by the arrival of two boys. The older one had been saddled with an acne-riddled face and dragged his younger brother by the ear. These were Lilah's boys.

"I'm ready to leave," the older one announced to his mother, ignoring Agnes entirely. "You said this wouldn't take long and I'm supposed to meet my friends tonight!"

"Oh, we can't leave yet," Lilah explained. "I still have to find the doctor and convince him to put me in the finals. Why don't you head home and leave Joe here? Agnes will watch him, won't you?"

Agnes, who had been attempting to slip away, stopped half out of her seat. "I'm sorry, Lilah. I just told you I had to leave. I've left my rabbit home alone."

"Nonsense." Lilah laughed. "you can't have been planning to leave before the announcements. No, Agnes. You can watch Joe for a couple minutes for me while I go find the doctor, and Brandon can leave to hang out with his friends. It's the perfect arrangement."

The acne-covered teenager vanished before Agnes could object. The younger boy, Joe, stared up at Agnes.

"Hi," she said.

He responded by making a fart noise with his mouth.

Lilah laughed. "Wonderful, see? He already likes you. Don't worry, Agnes, I'll be back in a jiffy, and watching Joe will be good practice for if you ever have your own."

With that, the nurse vanished, leaving Agnes stranded with a child, and very much unable to leave.

Chapter Thirteen

MURDER BUNNY

While Agnes was out, I spent the night with my paws up on a sofa, wrapped in a tiny robe that I pulled off one of Agnes' stuffed animals, enjoying a thimble of sweet, red merlot.

No, that wasn't entirely true. Enjoying was a stretch. I usually drink scotch, and preferably nothing less than 16-year Laphroaig, but Agnes' palate wasn't so refined. So I was making do with the wine. I figured if I drank enough of the stuff, the taste would become more palatable.

Later, I found myself growing quite hyper. Some might even have said tipsy, but that's unconfirmed. To me, there wasn't any reason for it except for a sudden, joyful awareness of my evening's freedom. I kicked the stereo on and spun the radio dial until that sound of old-time rock 'n' roll filled the house. It felt like living in a movie. Soon I was dashing like a maniac around the house.

That's when I discovered that Agnes really is living in a time warp. Her house feels like a relic from the Victorian era. Every room has at least two pieces of broken-down furniture (I counted) and it smells like old creams and burnt cakes. I must say that the whole effect is more than a bit off-putting.

I was curious about the attic, so I hopped up onto the bookshelf in the spare room and leapt onto the cord that dangled from the ceiling and clung to it. No use. I don't weigh enough to tug open the attic hatch, so I just ended up sliding down the cord and dropping to the floor.

Then I poked my nose into the upstairs bathroom. It was entirely decorated in pink. There was ripped pink gauze drapery, pink rugs, dirty pink tile, faded pink hand towels. This felt like ancient decor, and not in a good vintage way. I wondered how long Agnes had been living here, and what was keeping her from putting her own mark on this house.

Finally I scurried into the master bedroom. There was an old-timey oval stand-alone mirror in one corner. An unmade bed was decomposing in the middle of the room with two stacks of dusty hardcover books teetering on either bedside table. I steered clear of those because one jolt and they could snuff my little life out. Worst of all was the clothing. There were dresses, blouses, skirts, underwear, all strewn across the floor and piled on the Victorian dresser. She could've fueled sales at a thrift shop for years with this collection alone.

The door to the closet was open but it was so thick with fabric on the floor that I didn't dare to explore inside. One wrong step and the next person to see me would be the real estate agent who would discover my skeleton buried beneath a pile of discarded hats. Also, I didn't know if the clothing belonged to Agnes or to her grandmother. It was hard to tell, really. The two had blended together.

She was single, I knew, and truth be told I couldn't imagine her otherwise. She was pretty enough to attract a gentleman caller, to woo a suitor. But part of me wanted to teach her how to rearrange herself, her clothing, her life. Even in the two days since I'd chosen her, I could see that she was fairly hopeless at anything remotely social.

Plus, remember that I'm a bunny. If a small furry mammal

wants to give you dating advice, consider yourself in real trouble.

But that didn't matter to me, since my overriding purpose here was to use Agnes as my proxy. She was going to help me find Nigel's murderer.

I hopped downstairs to the living room and jumped onto the window sill. From here, I could see the neighborhood. I didn't care if the neighbors could see me. Cats do this all the time--why couldn't bunnies?

I watched the traffic passing along the street. Just to my right was Nigel's house. If I squished my whiskers up against the corner of the glass, I could make out the gingerbread Victorian molding and the high porch with the wicker outdoor loveseat. I remembered seeing Nigel out there on warm nights and felt a small tear trickle out of my eyes. I hated when I cried because the fur always came away matted.

Then, through my blurry eyes, I saw something suspicious.

It was a dark figure, prowling around the side of Nigel's house. It was a man, I could tell, but he was dressed entirely in black, even to the mask wrapped around his face. He was feeling the outside boards, as though looking for something-- a weakness, perhaps.

I didn't know what to make of it.

Then I saw the man reach up to the side window. It was the one in the kitchen, over the sink. He tried to open it but it didn't budge. Then he reached into his pants and removed what looked like a small crowbar. He slipped it under the window and jimmied it around for a while. Then he reached up, lifted the window open, and pulled himself into Nigel's house.

This was a break-in. To my former home.

I started to panic.

Chapter Fourteen

AGNES

Agnes rushed through her front door and slammed it shut behind her. The loud noise made her feel guilty, and she glanced towards the stairs, half-expecting her grandmother to be there, wagging a finger at her for damaging the hinges.

Of course there was no ghost, only little Marshmallow, hopping excitedly up and down on the stairs. Maybe he was scolding her as well, in his own way.

"I had to do it, Marshmallow," Agnes explained, brushing her loose hair out of her eyes. "I just want to slam the door on this entire night and forget it ever happened."

Agnes leaned against the front door and slumped down. It was a tad overdramatic, but it felt good to pout. After all, she'd spent most of her evening wiping boogers off a bratty kid who'd yanked her hair and wiped banana pudding all over her grandmother's nice dress.

"I've no idea how to get this stain out," she moaned. "And the worst part is that I ruined my night for nothing. I was no use to Esther at all. I could've just curled up on the couch with a nice cup of tea, a good book, and my sudoku puzzle for afterwards."

Marshmallow bounced along the floor towards Agnes. His usual scurry was now a set of unusual hops that took him leaping higher into the air than normal, while propelling him forward very little. He must have been very excited to see Agnes.

"We could even have cuddled together on the couch while I read. Wouldn't that have been nice?" She patted the ground beside her, gesturing for him to come now. She would tickle behind his ear just how he seemed to like and tell him all about her problems.

Not that he would understand of course. Although, she couldn't shake the feeling that he might. There was something about her new pet that seemed unnaturally intelligent.

Certainly, he understood that she wanted him now, for he erratically jumped right to Agnes' hand.

"That's a good bunny," she told him fondly, resting her hand on his head and stretching her finger to find the spot he liked. "See? Wouldn't this have been a nicer night? Just the two of us."

Normally, once Agnes patted him how he liked, the excitable Marshmallow would settle and curl up in an adorable ball of fluff alongside her hip, pressing his little pink nose into her skirts while his back leg kicked in delight. Now, however, he refused to keep quiet.

Marshmallow kept leaping, his eyes coming level with Agnes' own. Their gazes met, and Agnes swore she recognized something in the bunny's large, blue eyes.

Fear.

"You're scared, aren't you?" Agnes asked, pulling her legs closer and pressing her back against the door, suddenly feeling anxious. "Has something happened?"

Marshmallow stopped jumping and his head began nodding, his ears swinging wildly.

"Oh dear." That was not comforting.

Agnes scrambled to her feet and began peering around the living room, trying to spy anything amiss. There was something gleaming on the floor in the living room, just by the couch.

"Is this it?" she asked, as she took a few steps forward and peered down to inspect the object. It was an old sewing thimble of her grandmother's. How odd. Agnes never touched the sewing stuff. Perhaps it had been stuck under the couch and only recently become dislodged.

She lifted the thimble and was surprised to find the inside damp. Something red came off on her finger.

"Oh no." A horrible thought occurred to Agnes and she looked worriedly towards Marshmallow. "Is this your blood? Did you cut yourself on this somehow?"

The bunny shook his head, ears flapping about once more. Then he started hopping again. He made his way towards the window near the front of the living room, bouncing onto the old brown armchair and then up to the sill. He pressed his face against the corner and then turned back to Agnes.

"You want me to look out the window? But what's happened outside that would scare you?"

Even though she didn't understand, Agnes followed Marshmallow. She couldn't fit on the sill, but had to squeeze behind the armchair so that she could press her face against the cold glass.

"I don't understand why you want me to do this," Agnes said, feeling silly with her nose smushed against the window.

But as she stared outside at the familiar street, she saw something that made her gasp.

There was a hole in one of Nigel's windows.

Someone had smashed the glass, leaving a jagged pattern, like an uneven twelve-pointed star that glistened dangerously in the streetlight.

"There's been a burglary, hasn't there?" Agnes said, staring at Marshmallow in shock as the rabbit began nodding frantically once more. "Oh my."

Things like that never happened in Warrenton. It took Agnes a few seconds to realize what the next obvious step should have been.

She slapped her palm to her forehead. "I have to call the police! But Marshmallow, you're the only witness. Do you have any clue who it is?"

The rabbit's ears lowered and his head hung down.

The no couldn't have been any clearer. He looked so down on himself that Agnes patted his little head before grabbing the phone. "Don't feel too bad. I doubt they'd have counted you as a credible witness anyway."

Chapter Fifteen

AGNES

A loud horrible beeping jolted Agnes awake the next morning. Beside her, Marshmallow sprang from her pillow, reaching a foot into the air.

After the police had left last night, Agnes had been quite shaken. The officers didn't seem too concerned about the burglary. In fact, most seemed to think it was probably some kids who'd thrown a rock, out causing trouble for no reason.

Judging from Marshmallow's reactions, however, Agnes could tell that wasn't the case. She'd struggled to fall asleep that night, and she'd let the bunny cuddle with her on her bed. At first, he'd resisted, but after a while, he'd curled up on the pillow and rested his little nose into the crook of her neck, ears perked up as Agnes read aloud from one of her grandmother's old books that were still stacked beside her bed. The two had fallen asleep like that sometime long after midnight.

Now, according to the clock, it was six o'clock in the morning. Agnes' fingers scrambled to find the off button, knocking the screeching beast on to the floor. She rolled out of bed to pick it up, but in her haste, she stepped on top of it.

There was a loud crunch. Agnes jumped, lifting her foot up quickly. "Ouch!"

When she looked down, she saw at her feet a massacre scene. Shards of red plastic, shimmering silver metal coils, and broken bronze bells.

Agnes glanced at Marshmallow, who had hopped to the edge of the bed and was looking down at the disaster.

"At least it's off?" she said, giving him an apologetic smile and shrugging her shoulders.

He raised his ears, gave a little sniff, and then retreated back to the pillow.

"You've got the right idea," Agnes said, rubbing her eyes. She was exhausted. There was no way she could get to work on time. She needed a few extra hours of rest, or she would fall at the desk while stamping books.

Agnes picked up the phone from the bed stand, careful not to topple the collection of hardcovers, then crawled back into bed. "Esther will understand. I was up late dealing with the police. That's hardly the norm."

She addressed her concerns to Marshmallow, but he wasn't listening. He wagged his tail at her and burrowed his butt deeper into the pillow.

"Thanks for the pep talk," Agnes said.

She dialed her boss' number. It took a few rings before Esther answered. "Well, let's hear it then."

The librarian's cold tone made Agnes nervous. She licked her lips and curled her legs closer to her. "I don't mean to bother you, but there was a break-in at Nigel's house last night and I was up late dealing with the police. I was hoping I could come in later this morning?"

"Oh." Esther got silent on the other end of the phone. She sniffed. "Take the day then. Or the entire week, I suppose. Honestly, Agnes, I'm not certain why you even have the job. You certainly don't seem to care about it."

That wasn't fair. Being an assistant librarian might not have been Agnes' dream job, but she did enjoy it. Sorting books gave her a chance to skim through different titles and get a taste for different genres. Plus, there was nothing as enjoyable as pairing people up with the right stories, and hearing how much they enjoyed it when they returned the title.

"Is this because you're angry about last night? Esther, I'm so sorry. I told you, I'm just not good talking to people like that. It's really not my forte."

"Nothing is, Agnes. That's the problem."

The bluntness of her boss' statement stung. Agnes blinked back tears, uncertain what to say. Finally she stammered, "I'll see you tomorrow, all right?"

Esther sighed, but her voice remained cold and distant. "And for as long as we have the funds to pay for your job."

The librarian hung up before Agnes could think of a response.

Feeling sad from lack of sleep, anxiety over the break-in, and now disappointment in her work failure, Agnes slid under the covers and wrapped them tight around her.

"At least I've got you, Marshmallow."

The bunny twitched his ears and inched closer, resting his chin on Agnes' shoulder in agreement.

———

Feeling that it would be best not to wallow, Agnes forced herself to go visit Cindy later that day.

She sat on her friend's couch, a cup of tea cooling in her hands, while Cindy argued with a salesperson in her kitchen. She'd promised Agnes it would only be a minute, but she'd been on the phone now for almost half an hour. Cindy's feet tapped against the hardwood floor as she paced and her voice had gotten so high and shrill that Agnes expected the neighborhood dogs to start howling any second.

Agnes was glad that she hadn't brought Marshmallow. It might've damaged his poor ears.

In fact, earlier that morning, when Agnes had gotten out of the shower, she'd found the bunny sitting in his carrier. She would have been happy to bring him. She quite liked his company. But when she'd told him they were going to see Cindy and her daughters, he'd bounded out of the carrier and hidden under the bed.

"Aunty Agnes!" a little voice cried.

It was Rebecca, Cindy's youngest daughter. She and her sisters were in a cluster at the top of the stairs, with Fran and Josie standing behind Rebecca. They looked at Agnes for a tentative second before they all began to rush down the stairs.

"I'm not..." Agnes began to object, but she changed her mind. "Hi, girls."

No wonder Marshmallow was afraid of them. Though Cindy's daughters were sweet, when they moved in a group, they morphed into something monstrous. They were upon Agnes in a matter of seconds. Six loud feet bounding across the floor, six hands flailing and reaching towards her. Three mouths all showing their teeth in large grins.

Rebecca pushed her way onto her lap, wrapping her arms around Agnes' neck. Josie shoved herself into the chair alongside them, forcing Agnes into a corner. Fran perched on one of the arms, towering over them all.

"Did you bring us the rest of the cookies?" Josie asked, tugging on the sleeve of Agnes' white blouse, and staring up at her with large green eyes.

Fran answered the question before Agnes could. "Obviously, she's still not feeling well," she explained, tsk-ing at her sister the way an adult might.

"No, I'm fine," Agnes objected, wondering what had caused Fran to jump to that conclusion. Did she really look that terrible? She thought she'd caught up on the sleep she'd missed, and now that she was out of her house, her anxiety about the break-in was fading.

Ignoring Agnes' comment, Fran patted her head the way one might a small child. "Don't worry. We'll have to come and bake with you when you're better instead."

"Yes, okay." Agnes felt oddly embarrassed. It was strange having a ten-year-old treat her like a small child.

"Oh–I made you something!" Rebecca said. She leapt off Agnes' lap and rushed over to the corner of the room, where there was a plastic table full of craft goods. The girl carefully drew out a card from a small stack and crossed the room again and presented it to Agnes. Her eyes were wide with anticipation.

"Well, thank you very much," Agnes said, uncertain what else to say.

Cindy returned to the room. "Girls, would you all leave your Aunt Agnes alone? She's had a very stressful day. Go upstairs and play."

At their mother's command, the three girls vanished almost as quickly as they'd appeared.

"Sorry that took so long," Cindy said, settling back on the chair opposite Agnes. "You know how persistent some sales-people can be. I just couldn't get him off the phone. You were saying that you'd been so scared you imagined the rabbit was trying to communicate with you?"

"No, I..." Agnes shook her head. That wasn't what she'd been saying, but Agnes was too distracted to argue. She stared at the card in her hands. It had a large smiley face drawn on it, with thick red lips and pink eyes made of glitter, a combination that reminded Agnes of a delightfully cheery demon.

But the unnerving face wasn't what was bothering Agnes. Written with a black marker in a child's large, uneven writing were three words:

GET WELL SOON

"Isn't she sweet?" Cindy said, smiling as she noticed the card that Agnes was holding. "Becca made that for you after we saw you last time."

"But I wasn't sick," Agnes said, feeling confused.

"Oh, I know." Cindy nodded, picking up her cup of tea and taking a sip. She waved her hand as she spoke, as though she were searching for the words and plucking them out of the air as she found them. "But you know how you are, Agnes. The kids assumed you weren't well. I didn't know how to explain that some people are different."

Cindy stared at her. She seemed to be waiting for a response, so Agnes nodded uncertainly. "Oh, of course. Right." But inside she felt somewhat defeated.

That seemed to satisfy Cindy. "Okay, now tell me more about Nigel's old rabbit," she said. "If he's behaving funny, I'd be happy to take him off your hands. Josie and Becca think he's the absolute cutest thing in the world, and I imagine he poops less than a puppy."

Cindy continued to talk about how much her daughters would love a pet, but Agnes found it hard to concentrate. She nodded and hummed when it was appropriate, but she couldn't stop staring at the card. The message seemed to taunt her as Agnes tried to work out what it was about her that made children assume she wasn't well.

Chapter Sixteen

MURDER BUNNY

I sat in the corner of my cage, nibbling nervously on my own foot. She wasn't listening to me, and there was nothing I could do about it.

I'm referring to Agnes, of course. I didn't know any other human females, and at this point I wasn't quite sure that I wanted to. After all, Nigel had been murdered, nobody knew who did it, or even that it had happened. I'd been trying to point Agnes' thick skull towards the fact that I saw, with my own two side-mounted eyes, an intruder breaking into Nigel's house.

But no. In return, I received several things. First, I got a condescending pat on the head. Then I got to watch the police officers politely dismiss the incident as "boys with a rock", which wasn't even remotely close to what happened. Then, when I was clearly running in circles that night trying to make my point—no idea why she didn't understand that particular bit of communication—Agnes took me into her bedroom and read from one of her grandmother's old fusty Victorian books, trying to calm me down.

It worked. The story was all about a formerly wealthy family in 1930s England, living on their fading estate in the rural Cotswolds, the scenes filled with maids whispering gossip in kitchens and grown children being sent off to war and sickness befalling everyone. I was asleep in minutes.

Now, however, I've become angry once again. Justice has not been served. Nigel is still dead and we don't know his perpetrator. And nobody's listening to me.

It's enough to drive a bunny to madness.

I put down my paw. I'd always had the bad habit of biting on my own feet when stressed. It's a gross habit, especially because I'm sometimes forced to step in some unsavory liquids. Humans have really conquered the universe in that regard. Your shoes and boots and sandals aren't overrated.

The cutesy method of warning her wasn't working. Relying on subtlety, reading between the lines, had failed. I needed to be direct. It's not my nature but desperate times call for desperate measures. She needed to know that Nigel was murdered.

My nose twitched as I struggled in vain, looking for a way to relay my message. I looked around. The living room was a mess of stacked hardcovers, piles of grandma's old clothing, and rolls of brightly colored yarn.

Yarn.

I grew still. That could be the answer. My nose twitched as a plan began to cook inside my head.

I unlocked my cage and hopped over to the living room floor. The carpet was a dirty beige that hadn't been changed since the days of tea-length skirts, so I needed a color that would contrast with that. I nudged the red spool of yarn until it was upright, then found the end of it and gripped it with my teeth and ran across the living room.

It unspooled nicely. I measured a nice length, then

chewed it off quickly. Using my paws, I arranged the piece of red yarn into the shape of an N.

Then I chewed off another piece of red yarn, and arranged it into an I, next to the N.

I did this again, and again, and again. When I was finished, I admired my handiwork.

Spelled out nicely on the floor were three words:

NIGEL WAS KILLED

I made a quick little bunny hop in the air. That had been easy. Now all I had to do was wait for Agnes to come home.

I heard a car pull up in the driveway, the engine shut off, and a door thump shut. I leapt to my customary place on the window sill.

It wasn't Agnes. It was an old brown pickup truck, shot through with rust spots, its bed filled with a pile of dirty tools.

And coming up to the front door was Uncle Curtis, in that lazy, lopey walk that he had.

I squeaked. Of all people, he should not read the words I'd spelled out on the floor. I didn't trust him, not at all.

I raced down to the floor and began scooping up the bits of yarn with my teeth. I heard him coming in the front door. I pulled up the last letter as he entered the room, his dirty work boots directly at my eye level.

I sat stock still, completely wrapped up in red yarn. He looked down at me.

"You are one weird creature," Uncle Curtis said.

I admit it probably looked that way to him.

"What are you doing outside of your cage anyways?" He reached down and scooped me up. My body shuddered at the feel of his fingers on my neck. I found myself being carried back to my cage, then thrust inside. The cage door clicked shut.

"You stay there. You hear?" he said.

I don't know if he saw it, but I nodded. It was a lie. I wouldn't stay there one minute longer than necessary.

Chapter Seventeen

AGNES

Her time at Cindy's house had done nothing to cheer Agnes up. If anything, it had had the opposite effect. Now, not only was Agnes guilty about having disappointed Esther, she was worried about what her friend's comment had meant.

But you know how you are, Agnes.

Only Agnes didn't know. Sure, maybe she was quieter sometimes, but that wasn't a bad thing, was it? It just meant that she was a good listener, even if she did occasionally zone out and get lost in her own thoughts.

Or maybe Cindy had been referring to how clumsy she could be at times. Agnes didn't like that descriptor, but she couldn't deny it either. Had she dropped something when the kids were over last time? She didn't think she had, but it was entirely possible.

The more she considered it, the more depressed Agnes began to feel, but she had just the thing to cheer her up. The flour container that she'd ordered from the Batter Chatter should have come in today. The yellow daisies on the design would be just the thing to brighten her day.

Agnes parked outside the store and hopped out of her car.

She wouldn't dwell on what Cindy had said. It was only a passing comment, and Cindy probably hadn't known what she'd meant herself. She could've just been looking for an excuse for her daughters' strange assumptions.

———

The Batter Chatter was the center of the Warrenton baking community. Anyone in the region with a passing interest in the edible assortments of flour, butter, sugar, and eggs eventually made their way into its warm embrace.

Agnes went into the Batter Chatter and immediately felt lighter. Despite being a store, the room always felt warm and cozy. Today, it smelled like freshly baked apple streusel pies.

"Twice in one week?" Margie said, looking up and giving Agnes a motherly grin. "How lucky for us. Have you got Fluffy with you? I'll have to call Ashley out of the back. She'll be devastated if she misses him."

"No, he's at home," Agnes admitted, feeling suddenly self conscious. Didn't Margie know what she was here for? "I was just passing by and I thought–"

"–you needed some baking supplies?" Margie guessed, coming out from behind the counter. "I suppose you've got all of Dolores' old recipes, don't you? She was always very particular with her ingredients. If you tell me what you're making, I can give you some tips."

"No, no... I mean, thank you, that's very kind, but I'm not here for ingredients," Agnes stumbled over her words. "I thought you'd said you were getting a shipment with the flour container today. Did it come in yet?"

Margie's eyes widened, and her mouth opened in a small circle of surprise.

Agnes began to feel even more embarrassed as though she'd made a mistake. "Did I mishear you yesterday? Or am I

just too early? I'm so sorry. I should've asked what time ship-
ments come instead of just assuming."

"No dear," Margie reassured her, resting a hand on Agnes'
arm. "You're right. You wanted the one with the yellow
daisies, I recall. The only problem is that someone else
already purchased it. Sandra Dee was insistent that she have
it! And I knew you wouldn't mind."

But Agnes did mind. She'd specifically requested that jar.
Sandra Dee had been there then too. She and Margie both
must have known that Agnes wanted it.

However, Agnes didn't say any of that. Instead, she
said, "Oh."

It wasn't even a word. Just a single, pathetic, meaningless
syllable.

Margie smiled, seeming to take this as confirmation of her
earlier assertion. She took hold of Agnes' arm and guided her
to the counter, much like how one might a small child. "We'll
order you another one, shall we?"

"Will it come tomorrow?" Agnes asked. She allowed the
store owner to place her in front of the register. She stayed
there, standing, while Margie got back behind her computer.

"Oh no!" Margie laughed. "We can't afford to get ship-
ments every day! We get new kitchenware sent over every
other month."

"Oh." That syllable slipped from Agnes' mouth again. She
forced a weak, embarrassed laugh. "I guess that was a silly
question."

That wasn't what she wanted to say though. Agnes wanted
to tell Margie that this was ridiculous. It was poor business to
sell an item that one of your clients had put on hold, and
Margie wouldn't have done this to another one of her
regulars.

However, Agnes kept her thoughts to herself. Meekly, she

nodded to everything the store owner said and filed a request for another yellow daisy flour container. Then she smiled, thanked Margie, and left the store. She never expressed her annoyance. She wasn't even brave enough to express her disappointment.

Because that's just how you are, Agnes.

————

Agnes berated herself the entire drive home. Why was she so timid? She was always so concerned about upsetting other people or hurting their feelings, but what about her feelings? She mattered too.

She ought to turn around and go back to the Batter Chatter and quarrel with Margie. She did like Margie, however, and didn't want to offend her and have a messy confrontation. Maybe she could write her a letter instead.

However, as Agnes drove up to her house, all thoughts vanished from her mind, swept away by a sudden tidal wave of panic.

Her front door was wide open.

It was whoever had broken into Nigel's place. They were here! They were coming after Agnes next.

Her heart pounded in her chest. She should leave, but she was suddenly too scared to drive or to go inside. She needed to hide and hope they didn't notice her!

Agnes was about to curl into a ball and duck under her steering wheel when she saw the robber's head in her kitchen window. It was a man with dark hair.

It was Uncle Curtis.

The tension disappeared from Agnes' body, and she sighed in relief. Thank goodness!

But this wasn't a good thing. The annoyance that Agnes had been battling on her drive returned in full force, only now it was directed to her uncle. Why did he keep breaking into her house?

Agnes stomped out of her car and slammed the door behind her. She marched through her front door, taking a deep breath, preparing to shout louder than she ever had.

The wind was knocked out of her as she bumped into her uncle, who was exiting the kitchen with a bag of stolen food in his hand.

He didn't look guilty. He looked totally pleased to see his niece. "Great timing, Aggie, I was getting worried I was going to have to cook dinner myself. Why don't you whip us up something? You can manage at least eggs and toast, can't you?"

He laughed afterwards as though he'd said something hilarious.

It was more than Agnes could take. "Get out of my house!" she exploded.

The force of her voice shocked Agnes, and she was momentarily stunned by her own self-assertion.

Unfortunately, her uncle was not.

Uncle Curtis laughed. "Don't throw a tantrum, Aggie! You never bothered as a kid, terrible idea to start now you're all grown."

"I'm not throwing a tantrum," Agnes said, no longer screaming, but her voice still uncharacteristically loud. "This isn't your house. You don't have my permission to be here. Seriously, you need to get out."

"Or what?" her uncle snorted. "You'll call the cops? We both know you're not going to do that, Aggie."

"That's exactly what I'm going to do," Agnes said.

Uncle Curtis' eyebrows rose in surprise, but he didn't move. Maybe he thought his niece was bluffing. Calling the police and causing a scene wasn't her style.

But it was today.

Agnes stepped back and grabbed the portable landline receiver from where it was charging on a side table. Slowly, so her uncle could see the buttons, she dialed the number for the local police.

"All right, all right, don't be so overdramatic. I'm leaving." Uncle Curtis pushed past Agnes and hurried out the house. He took her food with him and closed the door on his way out.

Agnes bolted it shut behind him, and then made her way into the kitchen to inspect the damage.

Her call went through to the police. She heard the first ring in her ear.

Agnes had a decision to make now. She could hang up, which is what she would normally do, or she could report her uncle for the theft anyway. It was doubtful that the police would lock him up, but they might talk to him about it, and maybe that would make him think differently in the future.

She was debating between the two when she finally noticed Marshmallow hopping up and down at her feet.

"You're outside the cage again?" she said. "Poor thing. Did you get scared by the mean man? Don't worry, he won't be coming back here."

When she bent over to pet him, the bunny raced into the living room, turned, hopped once, and stood looking at her. Agnes guessed that he wanted her to follow.

She hesitantly entered the living room, the phone still tucked under her ear. On the other end of the line, a secretary answered. "Warrenton Station. How can I assist you?"

Agnes didn't answer. She gasped as she stared down at the carpet.

Written in red yarn on the carpet, in foot-high letters, was the message:

NIGEL WAS KILLED

Chapter Eighteen

MURDER BUNNY

My plan had worked like a charm. Agnes stood there gaping at me, then at the words on the floor, then back at me again.

"Did Uncle Curtis write this?" she asked.

I flung my head vigorously from side to side: *no*. Then, to add more emphasis, I ran back and forth, from left to right to left to right. It was probably more than necessary, but I didn't want my meaning to get lost in subtlety. There was too much at stake. A man had been murdered, a murderer was going to get away with it, and that couldn't stand.

Agnes still had the phone between her ear and her shoulder. "Yes, can you connect me with the medical examiner's office?" she said.

I realized that Agnes wasn't talking to me. So I began hopping up and down on her foot, insistently.

"I said that I would like to be connected with the medical examiner's office," she repeated. "The reason? Well, it's quite personal. Yes, thank you, I can hold."

She reached down and picked me up under the belly and carried me over to the sofa and set me down on the cushions. "Now behave," she said, tapping me on the nose.

By God, I could've bitten her. I felt a wave of sharp irritation sweep across me. I'd moved heaven and earth to spell out something this important, using yarn, and she just went ahead with her phone call, as if rabbits did this sort of thing *all the time*. Well, we don't. This was special.

She turned away, and I hopped down from the cushion and bounded across the room and blocked the doorway back into the kitchen.

"You are an exasperating little animal," she said.

I reared up on my hind legs and stood my ground and twitched my nose. When she reached down for me, I sprinted between her legs and back to the yarn on the floor. I began running in circles around it, just to emphasize the message here. Nigel had been killed. I was sure of it.

Finally, I threw myself onto the floor on my back, legs outstretched, mouth open. It was my best corpse pose.

"Now you seem to have died," said Agnes.

I sat up and looked at her. Then I looked at the red yarn, and finally back at her.

"I don't know how this message was delivered, or by who," she said, "but this invasive warning is the last thing that I need right now. Everything is just so *stressful*."

She plopped down on the floor, cross-legged, her long skirt falling in folds across the carpet. I ran over and flung myself into them, rolling around. It was one of my cutest maneuvers. Her fingers found my fur and as she stroked me, she seemed to relax.

Then Agnes grew stressed again as her telephone conversation restarted. "Yes, I'm here," she said.

I sat up and listened.

"Is this the coroner's officer? Yes? My name is Agnes Brooms and I was calling to ask if the autopsy on Mister Nigel Davies had been performed yet. No, I'm not a relative. I'm a concerned neighbor."

I saw her eyes go to the red yarn letters.

"Well, I have some questions about the death." She listened for a moment. "Oh, I see. When will the chief examiner return? Next week? No, of course, nobody wants to interrupt his vacation. I suppose Cancun is lovely this time of year."

She listened a bit longer. "So I'll just have to file a request. All right, that doesn't sound too unreasonable. What type of information can be released to me? Autopsy report and toxicology report only. Okay."

Her long front teeth bit down on her lower lip. I realized how much we had in common, her and me.

"Next Friday, I'll call back. Thank you very much," she said.

Agnes hit a button on the receiver and set it down on the floor.

Chapter Nineteen

AGNES

Agnes nervously rubbed imaginary bits of paper between her index fingers and her thumbs. How could Evan be so certain that Nigel's death was a regular heart attack when there'd been no coroner's report yet? What if there had been foul play?

The red yarn message burned like a fiery warning on her floor. She stared at the words, and remembered the break-in that had occurred at Nigel's house. What if they were connected? Something sinister really could be at play.

A high-pitched squeak escaped her lips. The idea of murder happening here in Warrenton was too much. It brought with it all manner of unpleasant questions, not least of which was this: *Who had left Agnes this message?*

There was only one other person who had been in the house that day.

"Uncle Curtis." Agnes groaned. She looked over to Marshmallow who was standing still as a statue, staring at her with big round eyes. "We think he did this, didn't he? But what would have possessed him?"

The bunny began stomping his back foot in response, his

mouth opening and closing in rhythm with it, almost as though he were trying to answer.

Agnes tried to help him out by guessing what he might say. "Maybe it was his idea of a practical joke."

The rabbit paused its stomping and stared at her in surprise.

Agnes smiled. Maybe she'd guessed what he was saying correctly.

"Knowing him, it might be," Agnes said, agreeing with Marshmallow, or more likely just agreeing with herself. She knelt down to begin unraveling the wool. "He's always had a weird sense of humor."

Agnes lifted the red yarn of the second 'R' and twirled it around her finger. The amount of yarn that had been used to create each word wasn't enough to repurpose into anything useful. Her grandmother would have been appalled had she seen this waste, especially given the tasteless message her yarn had been squandered for.

More than anything else, she couldn't believe her uncle's twisted sense of humor. This went way beyond the pale. He'd never done anything like this before.

Suddenly, Agnes froze. Her chest felt tight as she stared at what was left of the original message. What if it wasn't a joke, but a confession? Could Uncle Curtis have killed Nigel?

"No, no, no," Agnes said, shaking her head as she stared at the yarn. That couldn't be right. Her uncle was inconsiderate and uncouth, but he wasn't a murderer.

Marshmallow hopped over and began to push at the ball of yarn with his nose. He picked up a piece between his teeth, and Agnes had to pull it away from him before he ran off with it and made even more of a mess.

"It's not a toy," she explained to him, resting it back into the pile. "It's a joke or evidence or... I don't even know at this point."

The rabbit blinked at her for a few seconds before going back after the string.

Agnes sighed and scooped it back up before he could take it. She felt stressed and even more anxious than usual. Something strange was going on here, and she needed to get to the bottom of it.

She picked up the phone from where she'd rested it beside her and dialed her uncle's number. He answered on the fourth ring.

"Uncle Curtis," she said.

Agnes heard him snort at the other end of the line. "I'm back at my place," he said, "and I ain't leaving again for the night, so I hope you didn't tell the police anything different."

In the midst of everything, Agnes had completely forgotten that she was to report him to the police. "No, it's not that. I'm calling about the message you left me."

There was a loud slurping noise as though he were sipping something through a straw. "You mean that you're out of chips?"

"What? You didn't leave me any message about food." Agnes tried to keep the frustration out of her voice as she pulled the yarn away from Marshmallow yet again.

Another slurp. "Yeah I did. It's on the pad on the fridge. The one my mom used to use. It would help you get organized."

Agnes' jaw clenched. She knew the notepad her uncle meant. It hadn't been touched since her grandmother died, and the top page still had a short shopping list that had been written in beautiful cursive letters. Apparently, the notebook also now advertised Uncle Curtis' love of chips.

"I meant the message in the living room," Agnes said. Important as this conversation was, she was finding it difficult to focus. Marshmallow was hopping around, trying to take the yarn from her. The rabbit wouldn't shoo, no matter how much Agnes tried to move him.

There was no response on the other end of the phone. Then he simply said, "What?"

"You know, the message you left in yarn on the living room floor," Agnes said.

Uncle Curtis snorted. "I have no idea what you mean."

Agnes began to explain, but she paused. She wouldn't exactly have called her uncle a dramaturge, but he sounded genuine. However, that didn't make sense. Her uncle had just been in the house, and he surely wouldn't have missed such a strange message.

"Afraid I dunno about that," Uncle Curtis said.

"You're telling me you don't know anything about a message on my floor?"

"Nope."

"Spelled in red yarn?"

"You mean like if I'd spun you a tale or something?"

"No–"

"Look, I just left you the one thing about chips, okay?" he said. "So gimme a call when you get 'em."

They disconnected, and Agnes was more confused than ever. If Uncle Curtis really hadn't seen the message on the floor, that meant that whoever left it had to come in after he'd left. But nobody had entered.

At least, no person had.

Agnes' eyes widened as she stared at Marshmallow. The bunny was the only one who'd been alone in the living room.

She lifted up one of the ends of the piece of yarn. Its ragged ends looked like it had been chewed through by a pair of incisors, not cut with a pair of scissors.

"It couldn't be," Agnes whispered to herself. Eyes still on him, she pushed the ball of string towards the rabbit.

The bunny hesitated, and Agnes wondered if she'd made a

ridiculous assumption. A second later, however, Marshmallow grabbed the piece of yarn in his mouth and took off running with it. He darted so quickly that it was almost a pity rabbits didn't compete in sports. As he scampered around, Marshmallow distributed the yarn in patterns.

Only they weren't patterns. Those were letters. She watched as the rabbit fixed back the word MURDER.

Then the truth hit her like a pile of carrots falling from the sky.

It was the bunny who'd spelled out that message.

Chapter Twenty

AGNES

Twin feelings of shock and excitement battled within her. Then the excitement won, and she leapt up from the floor.

"Wait," Agnes said, "do you understand language?"

Bunny nodded.

"Are there others like you?"

The bunny gave a little shrug of his shoulders.

"You're not sure. But how do you know Nigel was murdered? Why are you telling me?"

Agnes looked down at the bunny. His mouth worked itself as though he were trying to communicate. Given that he could spell out words with yarn, he probably was.

A laugh burst from Agnes' throat. She clapped a hand over her mouth to stop the next one from escaping. This wasn't funny, but then again she wasn't certain what other response was appropriate upon finding out that her new pet could write.

Marshmallow suddenly looked concerned.

Agnes inhaled deeply, then exhaled. "I'm sorry," she said, "it's just that this is a bit strange for me, you know?"

The rabbit nodded. It was probably strange for him too.

She wondered if he'd ever communicated with a human before.

Things were starting to click. She didn't know who the killer was, but she did understand why Marshmallow had wanted to find a way to tell her the truth.

"You don't know who did it, but you want to find out, don't you?" Agnes guessed. "And you want me to solve it."

Marshmallow nodded.

If the same thing had happened earlier that morning, Agnes would have probably told the pet no. After all, solving crimes was best left for the police. However, given the way that several members of the community had assured her that Nigel had merely suffered a heart attack, and given the new fire that Agnes was feeling after confronting her uncle, she was feeling daring.

"Okay," she said, smiling at the rabbit. "I'm in. I'm going to help you. Together, we're going to figure out who killed Nigel."

There was only one problem with Agnes' bold promise. She had no idea how to go about solving a murder.

"I don't suppose you know who the killer is, do you?" she asked.

Marshmallow twitched his head first left and then right, almost as though he were smelling something on either side.

"That looks like a no," Agnes said. "Another question. Do you know where Nigel's carrot cake recipe is located?"

Marshmallow shook his head sideways again.

"Did Nigel write down his recipes at all?"

Again, the rabbit shook its head no.

"Okay," said Agnes, smoothing her dress out of nervousness, "forget the recipe for now. Do you have any idea who the murderer might have been?"

Marshmallow's eyes widened. He bounced up and down in excitement, nodding his head.

"Oh, excellent!" Agnes hadn't expected it to be that simple.

She stared at the rabbit, waiting for more of a clue. He stared back at her.

Agnes, you silly goose, she chided herself, *he can't talk.*

She laughed nervously. "Perhaps you can spell it out for me again? In red yarn?"

Instead, Marshmallow hopped towards the kitchen.

"Goodness, what are you doing?" Agnes asked, scrambling up from the floor so quickly that she almost tripped over her dress.

The bunny was leaping up and down in front of the counter.

"Do you want to show me something up there?" Agnes managed to catch him during the brief second that he was on the floor, then lifted him onto the countertop.

Marshmallow scrambled across the surface to the built-in shelf laden with books, jars, and trinkets.

"Are you looking for the flour jar?" Agnes guessed. She remembered that the bunny had come with her when she'd gone to The Batter Chatter. "I don't have the new one. Margie gave it away to someone else. Can you believe it?"

She'd hoped the furry prodigy might sympathize with her, maybe come over and give her an affectionate cuddle. But he kept jumping. Either he hadn't heard her, or he was trying to show her something else.

Agnes stepped closer to the rabbit and watched his movements. His front left paw was tapping at a leather-bound notebook. It was so old that the pages were yellowing and starting to fall out.

"That's my grandmother's old recipe book," Agnes said, picking it up off the shelf. Smiling fondly, she tucked some of the loose pages back in.

Marshmallow followed the book with his eyes. He twitched his ears at it, obviously trying to tell her something.

"I don't think this can help us solve Nigel's murder," she said. "It's just full of things to bake."

As soon as Agnes finished her sentence, the bunny started nodding his head.

"Is that what you want me to do?" she said. "You want me to bake?"

Marshmallow twitched his nose for a moment, then nodded his head.

Oh dear, Agnes thought. *Maybe we're not on the same page after all.* She couldn't see what baking had to do with Nigel's murder. Maybe her new pet was just missing his former owner.

"I can't make carrot cake like Nigel used to," she said. "At least, I assume his recipe was very good."

Agnes trailed off as the bunny leapt off the counter. He landed in a tight little ball and rolled, doing a somersault along the kitchen floor. It was an expert move. Then he scurried out of the kitchen.

She followed him, and in the living room she saw the rabbit standing on his hind legs, his front paws up on the coffee table. He was sniffing at a stack of books and papers.

"I meant to tidy those," Agnes explained. "I suppose I put away so many books at the library, I just don't want to put away any more when I come home."

Marshmallow bit down on one of the pieces of paper, then somehow managed to topple backwards. He landed on the rug with a surprised little squeak.

Agnes moved the books to see what was on the piece of paper that the rabbit had bitten. It was a bright blue flier with information about The Bake-Off. Marshmallow had nibbled off one of the corners.

Agnes understood. "I mean, don't get me wrong, I'd love

to enter this, but I doubt they're still taking entries. And anyway, I don't see what this has to do with Nigel."

The bunny stomped his hind leg and shook his head, annoyed.

"Oh dear. There's something I'm not getting, isn't there?" But this was too important to give up. "Are you suggesting the Bake-Off and Nigel's murder are connected?"

Marshmallow violently shook his head yes.

Agnes pursed her lips, thinking. Then she gasped, her eyes widening. "You think that it was another baker who killed Nigel, don't you?"

The rabbit leapt into the air once, the picture of excitement. When he came down to the floor, he stared at her.

She began pacing the room. "Of course! This makes sense. Nigel was the favorite to win the competition this year. One of the other contestants might've gotten jealous and snapped." Then the truth hit her. "That's why you want me to enter the competition! So that I can *spy* on them!"

Marshmallow tilted his head to the side, giving her a curious look.

"We'll have to go now and try to get in. I hope I'm not too late!"

Agnes scooped the bunny out and rushed out to her car. She put him on her lap and started the engine. She was halfway out of her driveway by the time she realized that it probably wasn't the best idea to drive with an animal on her lap. However, she didn't dare risk going back. If she slowed down or turned around, Agnes was certain she'd lose her resolve. After all, entering a baking contest and trying to solve a murder were both very large tasks, and ones that Agnes would usually shy away from.

But not today.

"Settle down, okay?" Agnes said to Marshmallow who

kept pawing at her, perhaps upset that he wasn't in his crate as well. "I have to focus on driving."

The rabbit must have understood the importance of that, for he lay down in her lap.

———

Agnes tried to formulate a plan on her way to town hall, where the organizers of the event worked. Of course, it would be too late for her to enter the Bake-Off as a competitor, and she doubted that she would have qualified for the contest at this point anyway. But perhaps she could sign up for some other job.

She arrived at the town hall and parked her car. It was too risky to leave Marshmallow alone in the hot sun, so she picked him up and carried him in her arms into the building.

Normally, the town hall was quiet, with each department staying quietly in its assigned area of the large building. The festival was its busiest time, however, and people were darting all around. The competition was being held in the local television studio and broadcast live, so there were ovens and baking stations set up for the event. Agnes knew that someone must be in charge of organizing all of that and getting all the ingredients.

Meanwhile, she herself was causing quite a stir. Quite a few people stopped when they saw the assistant librarian, wearing her grandmother's old pink dress, cradling a white rabbit in her arms.

One of the women, a thin blonde dressed in tall black stilettos, clicked over to Agnes. It was Monica Duncan, the mayor's secretary. They'd been childhood acquaintances; Monica's mother had been friendly with Dolores, Agnes' grandmother, and the two girls had been brought together to play a few times. They'd tolerated one another, but they'd never become friends.

"Agnes Brooms, what are you doing?" Monica hissed, her voice annoyed and shrill despite the polite smile on her face. "You can't bring a *rabbit* into the town hall."

"Oh," Agnes said, fighting back the urge to apologize. "Well, I won't be long, Monica. I'm just looking for the organizer of the Bake-Off. Do you know who that is, by any chance?"

Still keeping the strange, unfriendly smile plastered to her face, Monica managed to make a noise that was midway between a sigh and groan. "The mayor is managing the contest himself this year, and I assure you that he doesn't have time for you right now. Even if you are in the contest."

"But it's important," Agnes started to say, then stopped. She couldn't have heard that right. "Sorry, but did you say *I'm* in the contest?"

She felt Marshmallow wriggle in her arms, and the tips of his ears tickled the bottom of her chin as they perked up.

"Yes," replied Monica, "all of the former competitors are. It was just announced, and it's posted on the wall."

"But I've never been in the Bake-Off," said Agnes, feeling confused.

Monica grew exasperated and the smile disappeared from her face. "So here's what happened. Because the usual preliminary judging has been canceled due to Nigel's death, Mayor Greenberg decided to select former competitors for this year's competition. But Mayor Greenberg didn't remember that your grandmother had died. He demanded that Ms. Brooms be placed on the list, and nobody wanted to tell him that he'd made a mistake. Since you're the only Ms. Brooms left alive, you were automatically entered into the competition. See for yourself."

Monica pointed towards an official list that was pinned on a corkboard on the wall.

"It's a bureaucratic mixup. Don't question it, or else I'll be tempted to flag you." Her eyes landed on Marshmallow. "Now get that animal out of here, Agnes. Good heavens."

Agnes hurried over to read the announcement, still trying to wrap her mind around what had happened. Right there, clear as day on the notice listing the competitors, was her name: *Agnes Brooms*.

And below it, listed in alphabetical order were her four prime suspects.

Chapter Twenty-One

AGNES

If Marshmallow's hunch was correct, then Nigel Davies had been murdered by Lilah Dorchester, Sandra Swat, or Sebastian Monroe. The fifth competitor was Margie from the Batter Chatter, but Agnes was confident that they could rule her out. Despite the fact that the shopkeeper had sold Agnes' special order flour jar, Margie was too sweet to be a killer.

Of course, Agnes wouldn't have expected any of the others to be capable of murder either. Pettiness and back stabbing, certainly, but actual murder? However, she hadn't seen Sandra or Sebastian at the party the night that Nigel's house had been broken into. She also had to wonder where Lilah had disappeared to after she'd saddled Agnes with her awful kid.

Agnes would have to investigate all three of them, but she needed a plan. Or rather, they needed a plan.

———

The next day, Agnes brought Marshmallow to the library with her. She rested his crate on a table near the door where he could see everything that happened. "You keep an eye out just in case one of them comes in. Stomp your foot or something if I'm busy."

The rabbit nodded in agreement, and Agnes set about her usual job, stacking and reorganizing the books so that they were all in their proper place. She paid extra close attention to who had checked out what title. There was nothing suspicious under Sebastian's or Lilah's name. Sandra Swat, however, had recently borrowed a book called *The Baron's Murder*.

While filing everything away, Agnes also came across a book that might be useful to her. It was a nonfiction police procedural written by a retired officer, which detailed the investigation into a string of prolific murders that had taken place in a small town back in the seventies.

Agnes was leaning against one of the shelves reading the text when Esther spotted her. The older woman had her hair up in a loose silver bun, and her lips were turned down in the usual disapproving expression they wore when she caught her employee reading.

"Don't worry, it's my lunch break," Agnes assured her, addressing the concern before her boss had a chance to speak and pointing up at the large clock on the far wall of the library.

Esther paused, looking surprised by the statement, but she recovered quickly. "I know that. I just wanted to remind you that you have to file the books away from yesterday as well as this morning. I know how you like to put these things off."

"Oh I've already done that," Agnes told her. "It was the first thing I did when I came in this morning. Plus, I went through the lists to check what books are late in being returned and added the money onto everyone's names in the system."

"You did?" Esther looked truly flustered now. "Well, that's great. Enjoy your break. By the way, what on earth are you reading?"

Agnes grew flustered. "I mean, it's just, I don't know, a police procedural, I guess, about—"

"No," Esther cut her off, "I'm familiar with the text, but *why* are you reading true crime? I've never seen you venture outside of the fiction section before."

Agnes lowered the book, and examined the puzzled expression on her boss' face. There was part of her that knew she ought to lie, but it was difficult when the only creature she could confide in was a sentient rabbit. "Can you keep a secret, Esther?"

The librarian gave her a wry smile. "We librarians know how to stay silent, Agnes."

"I think that Nigel was murdered, and I'm investigating it."

Esther's eyes went wide. "I beg your pardon? Because that's not a very funny thing to say. If Nigel was murdered, I think law enforcement would be looking into it."

"Only they're not, because they haven't got the autopsy report yet," Agnes explained.

"How do you know that?" Esther asked, shaking her head, but she didn't give Agnes time to answer before continuing. "And why in the world would you be trying to investigate even if someone did do something terrible like that to Nigel? I know I told you to try and be a bit more adventurous, Agnes, but playing make-believe detective is certainly not what I meant."

"Well, I called the police and asked them," Agnes said, trying to answer her boss' first question before addressing her later statements.

However, it was clear that Esther had stopped listening. Her mouth had pulled itself into a tight line, and her eyes stared at something over Agnes' shoulder. She heard a commotion.

Agnes spun around to see what it was. She was just in time to see Marshmallow streak past them across the carpeted floor of the library. Right behind the animal ran Cindy's three daughters in hot pursuit.

"Agnes Brooms, why is there a rabbit in my library?" As a librarian, Esther never raised her voice, but she had developed a talent for angry whispering.

"Because he's my rabbit."

Esther sighed. "I will make an exception to the rule this one time only. But why have you brought him here?"

"I have an excellent reason to bring him here," Agnes said. However, she could think of no excuse for bringing Marshmallow to work with her other than the truth.

"And what is that?"

"He's helping me investigate the murder," she said.

Chapter Twenty-Two

MURDER BUNNY

Call me a snob, but I'm of the firm belief that genealogical research is one of the most civilized things that you can do. After all, nothing is more important than staying connected with one's ancestors. Heritage is key to understanding one's place in the world. The Mormons know how to do it right. They have huge repositories of family data out there in Utah. Say what you want about them but I respect any group that respects itself.

Me, I'm a bunny. We don't keep genealogical data. It's a miserable fact of our lives. I like to think it's because we reproduce too quickly to bother keeping track.

But Agnes and I reasoned that there was a likelihood that whoever murdered Nigel may have had a grudge against him. In my limited experience, I've found that grudges last through lifetimes and even across generations of rabbits.

So we hit upon a novel idea: I would look up the ancestors of the three major suspects. I would see if there was any record of bad blood between Nigel's family and theirs.

It was a long shot, but I play the long game, despite my short lifespan.

———

I'd sneaked into the library with Agnes carrying me in a paper grocery bag. The carrier would've invited notice, I was too big for her purse, and her backpack was already filled with whatever odds and ends and bric-a-brac that Agnes thinks is important enough to haul around town every day.

So a doubled paper grocery bag it'd been. Not an especially dignified method of travel, but it was better than nothing.

She'd set me down in a remote part of the library stacks. "Meet me back right here in three hours."

I'd nodded eagerly.

"If you have to use the bathroom, try to go where it won't be noticeable."

What an insult. I'm a bunny, not a chimp. I know how and where to relieve myself. I'd arched an angry eyebrow at Agnes, but she hadn't noticed.

"And don't let anybody see you!"

———

For the next two hours, I'd occupied myself with flipping through the microfiches in the microfiche room. Nobody uses those anymore, so I had the room to myself.

I'd brought my little spectacles that I use when I'm reading small print. I love reading, but bear in mind that I'm almost always sitting on top of every book that I read. It's terrible for nearsighted individuals like me. The spectacles have been a lifesaver.

First I'd looked up Lilah Dorchester. The Dorchester family were original settlers of Warrenton, back in the eighteenth-century. They'd owned and sold almost every parcel of land in the area, including Nigel's land. Maybe there'd been some kind of bad blood between them and the Davies family.

I'd found a marriage, in the nineteen-sixties, between Nigel's aunt and one of the Dorchester fellows. It was a wedding notice in *The Warrenton Bugler*. Excited, I'd plunged down that rabbit hole right quick. It is after all my birthright.

The truth was more mundane. Nigel's aunt and Mr. Dorchester enjoyed fifty-six years of wedded bliss, with four children, the love of an entire community, and funerals that drew hundreds of people. Evil people don't draw that many people to their funerals. It had to have been a happy union.

I'd scratched the Dorchester family off my list for now. Strike one.

Sandra Swat's family was next, which proved to be a short investigation. Sandra had been an only child, and she'd moved to Warrenton as an adult. She had no family here at all.

Strike two.

I'd moved onto the third suspect, Sebastian Monroe. This would certainly prove more fruitful. He was a difficult man and his family were known for throwing theatrical fits of anger. I remembered Nigel muttering about Sebastian, specifically the word "impossible" used to describe his personality.

Looking at church records, I'd found that the Monroe family saw several of its babies die young in the last half century. That was interesting. Could there be any way to connect Nigel to those deaths? I knew that Nigel's older cousin, Dr. Ray Davies, was a pediatrician who'd treated most of the children in the town up until age twelve or so, when they'd shifted over to the grown-up physician, Dr. Ambrose. Everybody had Dr. Davies until then, and if anything was happening with the town's children, he knew about it. He'd been practicing for almost fifty years.

I'd sat back in the swivel chair and took off my spectacles and rubbed the fur around my nose.

Then I'd heard the patter of feet. It sounded like a small stampede. The door had flown open.

Three children had burst into the microfiche room, destroying my solitude.

"It's Marshmallow!"

My ears had gone flat. I'd flopped over and played dead. I remembered these monsters, waiting them out behind the couch. I didn't have that advantage this time. Here, in an enclosed space with nowhere to hide, the only way to survive a gang of sugar-high children is to not play at all. Pretend to be dead and wait for them to tire of you. The same as you would do for a grizzly bear.

I'd felt my body being squeezed, handled, flipped, tossed, kissed, cuddled, stretched, and fought over.

"Give him to me—"

"No, you just had him—"

"It's my turn—"

I'd squinted my eyes shut so they couldn't see the fear. I'm sure they felt my trembling.

Then a woman had come into the room. "What are you doing, girls? Leave the bunny alone!"

It'd been Cindy. I'd met her before. These three vicious hellions were her terrible offspring.

They'd dropped me, and I scooted out the door.

———

My escape from the microfiche room caused the brats to invent a new game. It was called Catch-the-Bunny-in-the-Library.

I'm not in the best shape, but I can run when called upon. That call came fast and furious and repeatedly. The three shrieking demon girls pursued me down every aisle, through every row, in every stack. I hopped through gaps in shelving, leapt over beanbag chairs, and dashed beneath the feet of people studying at carrels.

No use. The girls were like bloodhounds, if bloodhounds could run like greyhounds. These girls were fast. I couldn't shake them.

I decided to distract them with some artfully dropped pellets, right in front of the young adult section. That would occupy them for a while—they would think I was nearby—while I sought refuge in the reference section instead. They wouldn't find me there.

Wrong. Five minutes later, six small sticky hands tried to drag me out from my tiny dark space under the Encyclopedia Britannica. I barely escaped them, twisting and wriggling so much that they dropped me.

I dashed by Agnes and Cindy, who watched me in shock. Agnes was leaning on a book cart. Cindy was carrying a pile of books for checkout.

Cindy said, "Marshmallow is making an absolute nuisance of himself."

"I'm not sure I'd put it quite that way," Agnes said.

"But the girls love him!" Cindy added, beaming.

"I'm not giving him up, Cindy," Agnes said. "He's had a hard month. I think he needs stability."

"I'm not going to lie, bringing him to work is kind of amazing," Cindy replied.

"Well," Agnes said, "he's bored at home. He says he needs new books to read."

Cindy laughed. "Very funny. I like it! A bunny that can read!"

Agnes looked at her with seriousness in her eyes. "I'm not being funny. He likes to read. And he can write too."

Cindy's laugh caught in her throat. She tilted her head, unsure of what to make of this news.

"Is everything okay with you, Agnes?"

"Yes. Why?"

"Your mental health is all right?"

Agnes smiled. "It's never been better, Cindy."

She lifted an eyebrow, spun on a heel, and kept pushing her cart. I hopped after her.

Chapter Twenty-Three

AGNES

Agnes left the library, carrying Marshmallow in her arms. Behind her, she was aware of Cindy and Esther muttering to one another.

"They're talking about us," Agnes whispered to the bunny as she loaded him into the carrier in the backseat of her car. "But you know what? For once, I don't care. Let them think I'm crazy. They'll see the truth when we solve Nigel's murder."

The bunny nodded his head in approval.

Agnes climbed into the driver's seat, started the engine, and drove out of the library's parking lot. Her destination was the Batter Chatter.

"If we're going to catch this killer, we need to draw them out of hiding," Agnes said.

Something warm wriggled against her right elbow. Marshmallow had slipped free of his carrier and had climbed into the front. For a moment, Agnes was concerned the rabbit wanted to sit on her lap. Instead, Marshmallow planted his tail on the seat beside her, turned his head and stuck his nose in the air. It was a haughty gesture, and one Agnes thought she understood.

"You're right." She laughed. "We're partners. You should ride in the passenger seat."

Marshmallow's chin twitched in an approving nod, and one of his ears flopped to the side. It was the image Agnes would expect to find if she looked up *cute* in a dictionary.

"So, partner," she said, reminding herself to focus on the road and not her adorable co-detective. "How do you reckon I do this next bit?"

———

"I'll need five bags of your finest baking flour, Margie," Agnes announced, repositioning Marshmallow, so that she could hold him with one hand while pushing open the door to the Batter Chatter with the other. "I have a carrot cake to prepare."

Agnes froze for a moment as she saw the shoppers within. When she'd rehearsed this in the car for Marshmallow, she'd imagined her only audience would be Margie, but the Batter Chatter had more customers than usual. Only a few were faces Agnes recognized. There were quite a few visitors who'd come into Warrenton for the festival.

Performing had never been Agnes' strong suit. She'd once played a cloud in her elementary school's production of *Jack and the Beanstalk*. Instead of dancing, she'd stared in wide-eyed panic at the bright lights, knees trembling until the music had cued her exit.

Marshmallow tapped his front paw against her hand, nudging her forward.

The rabbit was right. Agnes wasn't six years old anymore, and this was important. She could do this.

Agnes took a deep breath, forced a grin, and strutted into the Batter Chatter.

"Are you sure that flour isn't too advanced for you?" Margie asked, coming out from behind the counter. "We've recently received a few boxed cakes that are very good."

Margie rested a hand on Agnes' elbow attempting to move her toward a section near the back of the store. Beneath the packages of premixed pastries, the shelves were full of colorful cookie cutters, mini rolling pins, and children's aprons. A little girl plucked a kit labeled *My First Baking Kit* from the bottom and rushed to find her mother somewhere in the aisles.

Being directed to the children's section made Agnes flush. She wanted to mumble a *thank you*, slink to the boxed cake, and hurry out of the store before anyone else noticed. But Marshmallow's warm fluff snuggled against her arms as the bunny looked into her face. His nose twitched. He seemed to say, *Are you really going to take that?*

"No, I will not," Agnes answered, voice bursting through her embarrassment louder than she'd intended. But that was a good thing. The eyes of the shoppers turned to her once again. "I have a special recipe that I intend to try. It belonged to my dear neighbor, Nigel Davies."

To the out of town guests, this statement meant little, but Margie's eyes widened. Ashley stepped out from one of the aisles, followed by Sandra Swat.

"How do you have Nigel's prized carrot cake recipe?" Sandra asked. Her voice was shrill.

"He shared it with me before he passed away," Agnes said, voice dipping in volume. But she couldn't lose steam now. This was only half of the information she needed to relay. "And I intend to win the Warrenton Bake-Off with Nigel's carrot cake recipe on his behalf. So I'll be needing quality flour."

Sandra's mouth dropped open, like a fish.

Margie's eyebrows rose almost to her hairline. She sputtered: "But Nigel never—You can't—The contestants have already—"

"I can help you with that flour, Agnes," Ashley said, stepping forward with a smile. She patted her grandmother's shoulder, grabbed a basket from beside the door, and nodded toward the opposite side of the store. "Nan probably doesn't want to help you because she's competing as well."

Now that her performance was over, Agnes sighed in relief. The eyes moved off of her as she followed Ashley past a display of silicone utensils. But when Agnes glanced back, she found Sandra and Margie conferring in hushed whispers.

"I didn't think you'd entered the Bake-Off this year," Ashley said, stopping before the bags of flour. She took Marshmallow from Agnes' hands as she passed the basket, then cradled the bunny in her arms. "How did you manage to get into the final? Did you convince them with your cuteness?"

She addressed that last question to Marshmallow.

Agnes couldn't think clearly enough to explain. She was too overwhelmed by the wall of flours. Why were there so many types? Amaranth, rye, spelt, buckwheat, semolina, pastry, gram, potato starch—the options were nearly endless.

"I believe I can shed some light on the situation," a man's voice spoke a couple feet away.

Agnes turned and her newfound confidence threatened to collapse. It was Tobias Thornton, the antiques dealer who Esther had introduced her to at the party. Agnes had asked him for money with all the tact of a wet sock. She'd hoped she'd solve the mystery of Nigel's death before having to face his judgment at the Bake-Off. But now, here he was, dressed in a crisp gray pants, silk shirt, and red tie, looking as impressive as he had at the event.

Agnes brushed Marshmallow's fur from her grandmother's old gingham skirt.

"Ms. Brooms' place in the competition was a mix-up on my part," Tobias explained, smoothing the edges of his goatee. "We met the other night, and when I saw the list of previous winners, I mistook her for her grandmother. I'm pleased to run into you again, actually, as I was hoping to apologize. I don't imagine you'll want to compete." As he spoke, his eyes landed on the bunny in Ashley's hands. His eyebrows rose. "Is this the rabbit you told me about?"

"Yes, that's Marshmallow," Agnes said, uncertain whether to be delighted or horrified that the antiques dealer remembered her babbling about the bunny. "He's very clever."

"And adorable," Ashley added, booping the bunny's nose.

"Indeed." Tobias agreed, holding out his hands to take Marshmallow. Ashley reluctantly parted with the bunny. The antiques dealer lifted him up, and the bell clinked on Marshmallow's collar. Tobias stared at the bunny. Marshmallow stared back. Both seemed uncertain what to make of the other.

"Very cute," the antiques dealer said, and passed Marshmallow to Agnes as though they were playing a game of hot potato. Tobias seemed more polite than fascinated by rabbits. "I do hope you'll stay in the competition, Ms. Brooms. Errors can be providence, and I'm sure you've inherited your grandmother's skills."

"Thank you, Mr. Thornton," Agnes said, taking the rabbit. She felt genuinely appreciative of the compliment.

"But I have a question. Nigel never wrote down his recipes. How did you get a copy of his?"

It was the same thing that Sandra had just asked. "I can't reveal my secrets," said Agnes. "You'll just have to wait and taste it for yourself."

The antiques dealer huffed and walked away. Agnes wasn't sure whether he believed her or not. But she did feel more confident as she took three bags of cake flour up to the register.

Chapter Twenty-Four

MURDER BUNNY

On our drive back home, sitting in the passenger seat next to Agnes, I felt sweat break out onto my fur. My heart rate quickened.

I was having a terrible crisis of conscience.

I'd revealed my deepest secret to Agnes. I'd shown her that I could read and communicate with her. Now I'd changed her entire view of the world. It was like I'd tried to reveal that aliens were real. I know that no matter how many books or animated movies or television programs she has consumed, a talking animal is the stuff of fiction.

But I'd shown her that I'm not fiction.

I'm real.

To Agnes' credit, she seemed to be handling the discovery better than most people would.

"Marshmallow, did you see how Sandra followed me around the store?" Agnes asked, voice animated as she cranked the steering wheel around and accelerated down the street. "Do you think she was trying to see what ingredients I purchased for Nigel's carrot cake?"

I twinkled my nose and nodded so she'd know I agreed. Like any master detective, I'd kept a close eye on our suspects. Sandra Swat's suspicious behavior had been obvious. But what about Margie? Agnes didn't have the owner of the Batter Chatter on her suspect list. But Margie was a contender for the golden spoon as well. I supposed it was possible that her cheery demeanor was hiding a sinister killer. She'd certainly been quick to come and ring up Agnes' purchases.

The problem, as always, was how best to convey this information. My paws made writing with traditional implements a chore and typing all but impossible. Modern technological development simply doesn't consider rabbits in its design processes.

I hopped up and down on the seat, trying to attract Agnes' attention. When she glanced at me, I attempted to make an *M* with my ears. A simplistic solution, but sometimes those worked best.

"You look cute with your ears flopping over like that," Agnes said.

She was not getting it. I attempted to focus her attention on the shape by tapping them with my paw.

"Do you have an itch? I can scratch your ear—eek!" Agnes squealed, and her leg suddenly pressed against the brake. Her hand flung out just as I flew forward. She managed to stop me before I was unceremoniously dumped into the footwell of the vehicle.

The car halted with a slight bump. Agnes' hair covered her face, and her mouth was open in shock.

"Marshmallow! I'm so sorry," she said.

I was upside down. I could've righted myself, but it felt rather good to stretch my lower back. Flexibility matters as you grow older.

I felt her reach over and lift me out and soon I was being

clutched to Agnes' chest. Her face was buried in my fur. She was murmuring apologies.

I gave her a quick lick on her cheek. Just enough so she knew it was purposeful.

"Oh, thank you for understanding," she said. "I can't believe it. That driver cut me off and then I hit him."

I turned my head. Through the windshield I saw the front of her car was lightly touching the back end of a sedan. The sedan's driver's door was opening,

"Well, I hope he's not too upset," she said.

But the driver wasn't a he. I saw the distinct shape of a large woman stepping out, a huge mass of curly auburn hair that seemed to bounce like springs in a halo around her head. My tiny jaw dropped open.

"Oh, it's Marie!" Agnes said.

Marie had gone to elementary, middle, and high school with Agnes. She was a ton of fun, as long as you could tolerate her flair for the dramatic.

"Agnes Brooms!" she shouted.

Eek. Marie was going to think Agnes had been holding me while driving.

I leaped out of Agnes' hands and hopped into the back-seat. I hid behind her seat while the two of them spoke.

"My goodness, Agnes," Marie said, "I thought we would run into each other, but not literally!"

"It was completely my fault," said Agnes.

"Oh," said Marie, clutching the back of her neck, "it hurts, my poor neck! Why, you could've killed me!"

"I was going far too slow for that—" Agnes tried to interject.

"Nonsense! People can drown in two inches of water! My life could've ended just now!" She lifted a theatrical hand to her forehead. Then the woman's eyes fell upon me. I ducked my head down.

"Is that a rabbit in your vehicle?"

"Yes," said Agnes hesitantly, "it's Nigel's bunny. I'm taking care of him now."

"Oooooh," she squealed. She peered at me through the back window, tapping the window gently. "What a sweet little thing! What's his name? Never mind—I'm going to name him myself." She thought for a second. "I name you Sir Edmund Peabody the Magnificent!"

I curled up in the backseat and pretended to sleep, hoping Marie would leave. I don't care for anybody who tries to rename me against my will, especially when it's something that makes me sound like I'm pretending to be the fourteenth generation of landed gentry.

"Oh, poor thing, he must be tired," she said. Marie went back to Agnes' window. "So how've you been?"

"Everything is fine," she said.

"And your grandmother, how is she? She's such a sweetheart."

Agnes stammered. "Well, I mean, she's not with us anymore."

Marie staggered backwards, hand to heart. "No!"

"Yes, she passed on."

"Oh my goodness. You poor thing! Let me know if I can do anything to help. This must be so difficult for you!"

"It was a while ago," said Agnes. I could see she was uncomfortable. "Can I ask you something about Nigel?"

"Oh dear, if you must, I guess. Such a tragedy!"

"Did you notice anything unusual about Nigel in the days leading up to his death?"

"No! That's why I was so surprised when I found him! Aggie, let me tell you, I nearly fainted. It was one of the worst experiences—"

"What about the cake? Did it look like anyone had tampered with it when you found him?"

"Now that you mention it." Marie's eyes looked upwards. "There was frosting missing from the top of his cake. I remember because I thought that some kid must've been naughty and helped themself to a taste, and then Nigel probably saw it and the sight gave him a heart attack! I mean, you know he he was with his cakes!"

Agnes said, "You think someone swiped the frosting with a finger?"

"Yes, that's what it looked like! All over the top of the cake." Suddenly Marie looked at her wristwatch. "Oh! I'm going to be late. There's a summer garden party at the Wentworths starting in ten minutes and I promised them I would sing at least two classics to entertain the crowd. Mwah!" She made air kisses on either side of Agnes' face. "Toodles!"

"Bye, Marie," said Agnes. "And sorry again."

The woman ran back into her sedan, slipped into the driver's seat, and left the scene. The accident had been totally forgotten.

Agnes dropped her face into her hands. "My gosh, that was stressful." She looked back at me. I ran into the front seat and sat up straight and looked her in the eye. Then I twinkled my nose and lifted a paw. Hopefully she would know what that meant: I was listening.

"Marshmallow, I don't know if we're ever going to find Nigel's killer." She sighed, then looked at me again. "And how am I supposed to tell anybody the things that you've been showing me?"

She had a good point. I'd tossed a huge secret into Agnes' lap, and now she had to handle that hot potato the best way she saw fit. She was now a crazy person who owned a talking bunny rabbit. It was a spectacle she hadn't asked for.

It really was unfair to her. Every time I communicate information to her, she will have to invent ways to explain how she came by it. I didn't envy her the task. She doesn't have the luxury of being totally overlooked. I can testify to that personally. It's quite a relief sometimes.

Agnes was extra careful driving on the rest of the ride home. As for me, I dreamed of bringing her hands into my paws and reassuring her that we were fighting on the same team. I want Nigel's murderer to be caught just as much as she does.

Chapter Twenty-Five

AGNES

Agnes clenched her teeth as she attempted to saw through the carrot on the cutting board. Either the knives were dull or she needed to start lifting weights.

"I know carrot isn't your favorite, but we're going to mix in lots of lettuce and cucumber too," Agnes said. She peered over her shoulder to the small table in the center of the kitchen.

Marshmallow sat in its center, paper fanned around his paws. The pages were full of notes Agnes had made about each suspect. The bunny was reading them.

Even knowing what Marshmallow could do, the sight still shocked Agnes.

A circular chunk of carrot rolled off the chopping board and across the tiled floor.

"Five second rule. Plus, I'm going to boil it." She knelt down to grab the fallen carrot.

Marshmallow's ears rose. He looked up from the notes.

"What do you think?" Agnes asked, straightening up. "Sandra seems the most suspicious, don't you think?"

Marshmallow sat up on his haunches and raised his paw.

"Does that mean you agree?"

Marshmallow pointed toward something behind Agnes. She turned around.

On the stove, boiling water bubbled from her pot of pasta, spilling onto the electric burner and making it hiss.

"Oh no!" Agnes hurried to the stove and removed the lid from the pot. She tossed in the haphazardly chopped vegetables and stirred everything together with a slotted spoon.

"Do you think I should add salt and pepper? " She glanced over her shoulder at the rabbit.

Marshmallow twitched his nose. He tapped his paw against the pages. Evidently, the bunny thought there were more important things to focus on than dinner.

"Good point." Agnes left the pasta and vegetables to boil and took a seat at the table. "We've already determined that we need to look into Sandra Lee next, but we can't rule the others out. Do either of the other two suspects stand out? "

Marshmallow tapped Sebastian's page.

Agnes picked it up and considered her notes. It was no secret that Sebastian and Nigel had disliked one another. Sebastian managed a high-end furniture store near the center of downtown Warrenton. Nigel's antiques store sold many similar items. Whenever somebody needed a lamp or a new chair or a piece of unique decor, Sebastian would attempt to upsell them on a modern aesthetic while Nigel boasted about the value of vintage.

Beyond their career rivalry, the two men also competed in baking as well. Agnes had searched for records of the annual Bake-Off over the past ten years while she was in the library. Sebastian hadn't won since Nigel moved to Warrenton seven years ago. Was it possible that their professional rivalry had escalated into your true animosity? Maybe Sebastian had snapped and murdered Nigel in an attempt to steal his carrot cake recipe and finally win the Golden Spoon.

"He's definitely suspicious," Agnes agreed, tapping her fingers against the table. "What about Lilah Dorchester? She vanished from the party. I don't think we should dismiss her."

Marshmallow's head tilted in thought, but before he could communicate any theories about their third suspect, the phone rang.

The bunny's ears straightened. His eyes narrowed at the landline hanging on the wall in the kitchen as though personally offended by its interruption.

"Give me a second. I'll just check who it is in case it's the police calling to confirm that Nigel was murdered. "

Agnes got up and pressed the phone to her ear. "Hello, you've reached Agnes Brooms."

"Obviously, " Cindy's voice said at the other end. "Who else would it have been? You live alone. What are you doing tonight? "

"I'm inve–"

Cindy didn't wait to hear Agnes' answer. " I'll tell you what," Cindy interrupted. "You're having dinner with me and the girls. We're on our way to you now. "

Agnes frowned. It wasn't out of the ordinary for Cindy to invite herself over. She said it gave her an excuse to buy takeout and ditch her husband for a night. The intrusion didn't bother Agnes much when it was just her friend. But Cindy's daughters, sweet as they could be, had a tendency to get bored. Agnes didn't have toys or games for them at her house and Cindy never seemed to bring any. If the girls weren't entertained, they ran amuck through the house, rifling through the cupboards and drawers.

"Sorry, I can't tonight, "Agnes said.

"What do you mean? We're already on our way, and we bought you a hamburger. The girls are so excited to see the bunny. It's all they've been talking about. They've even chopped up some carrots to bring for him."

"He doesn't like carrots," Agnes muttered under her breath.

"What?"

"I said he doesn't like carrots," Agnes repeated more loudly. "And I'm sorry but I really can't entertain you or the girls tonight."

"Don't be silly, you don't have to entertain us. I'm going to watch TV. It's been ages since I had a chance to watch my shows. You know Scott hates when I put on any type of reality program."

"And will the girls sit on the couch and watch with you?" Agnes didn't know why she asked. She already knew the answer.

"Oh gosh no!" Cindy snorted. "Maybe Fran, but you don't have to entertain the others. Josie loves playing dress-up with your grandmother's old clothes, and Becca can play with your books."

"No, she can't. She colored all over my copy of *Sense and Sensibility* last time."

Cindy clicked her tongue. "You have three copies of that book, Agnes."

When there was no response, after a moment, Cindy sighed. "Well, read something with her then if you're going to be fussy. It's not like you have anything else you need to do."

"Yes I do!" Agnes tried objecting again. She didn't know how much clearer she could be. "I have other plans tonight."

"Really? With who?" Cindy sounded skeptical.

Agnes glanced at the bunny reading the notes on the table. "With Marshmallow."

Cindy laughed. "Your rabbit? Oh, I thought you were serious for a second. The girls love that bunny. They'll be delighted to spend time with him."

Agnes' hand tightened around the phone. Cindy wasn't listening.

"Cindy, you and the girls cannot come over tonight," Agnes said, struggled to get the words out. She hated saying no to anyone, but her friend was making it more difficult than necessary. "Marshmallow and I are solving Nigel's murder. We've got suspect notes everywhere, and I don't think that would be an appropriate conversation to have around your daughters."

Cindy was silent on the other end.

"Thank you for understanding," Agnes said. When there was still no response, she took a deep breath and hung up the phone.

Chapter Twenty-Six

AGNES

Agnes awoke the next morning feeling more excited and alive than she had in ages. Terrifying as it was to know that her neighbor had been murdered, trying to solve the crime quelled Agnes' anxiety and gave her a sense of purpose.

"Ready to investigate?" Agnes asked. She looked down at her partner. The bunny was nibbling a piece of lettuce on the living room carpet.

Marshmallow looked up at her with big brown eyes. He dropped the leaf back into his bowl and hopped toward her. Agnes bent over, scooped up the bunny, and placed him into the carrier over her shoulder. His nose twitched in objection.

"It's just to get you to the car," Agnes explained. "My hands are going to be full. "

Last night Agnes and Marshmallow had come up with a plan to stake out Sandra Swat's home. Warrenton was considered safe enough that people often left for brief periods without locking their doors. Agnes figured she could take a page from Uncle Curtis and do some snooping. It would be easy enough to lie and say she'd needed a bathroom if the hairdresser caught her. No one in town would suspect Agnes Brooms or her bunny of burglary.

Agnes wasn't entirely certain what evidence she hoped to find in Sandra's house. Perhaps the hairdresser had a shampoo full of poisonous chemicals. Or maybe there was a shrine dedicated to Nigel in her closet, full of images and recipes from his Bake-Off wins? Whatever evidence might exonerate or condemn Sandra, she wouldn't find it by hanging out in her own living room.

With Marshmallow slung over her shoulder, Agnes grabbed the supplies they'd prepared last night from the table beside the front door: a notebook and pen, two bottles of water, and a pair of binoculars. Heart pounding with both nervousness and excitement, Agnes turned the handle and stepped outside—only to find her path blocked.

Four people waited on her porch. Cindy stood before the door, fumbling through her purse. In a line to her left were Margie, Ashley, and a disgruntled looking Esther.

Agnes' brow furrowed. She glanced at Marshmallow and found him staring at their unexpected guests with the same confusion.

"What are you all doing—"

"Oh good! I was worried I was going to have to call you to let us in." Cindy pushed past Agnes into the house. "Why have you got your door locked? Don't tell me you really think there's a murderer on the loose? In Warrenton of all places!"

Agnes did think that. And given her ploy yesterday at the Batter Chatter, she'd made herself a target. If the murderer was after Nigel's carrot cake recipe, Agnes would be next on their list.

Before she was able to explain, the other three women on her porch followed Cindy inside. Esther, entering last, took Agnes' arm.

"Come along," Esther said, speaking with the exasperation that accompanied her tone whenever she spoke to Agnes. "We need to talk."

"But I haven't got time right now," Agnes tried to explain. "Marshmallow and I have a mystery to solve."

But the older woman dragged her through her own house toward the sitting area. Margie and Cindy took a seat on the tartan couch before exchanging a look.

"I told you, didn't I?" Cindy said.

Margie sighed and nodded. She turned to Ashley and raised her eyebrows. "Do you think you should...?"

The teenager looked up guiltily from her phone and slipped the device into her pocket. Then she jumped up from the old armchair, hurried over to Agnes, and gently took Marshmallow from his carrier. The bunny wriggled in her hands.

"He really doesn't have time to cuddle right now," Agnes said, interpreting Marshmallow's twitches. "We have somewhere that we need to be."

Ignoring her protests, Esther forced Agnes to sit on one of the chairs. She was surprisingly strong, despite being mostly bones.

"Listen, Agnes," Margie said, leaning forward with her hands clasped over her knees. She offered a sad sympathetic smile, the type reserved for old people with dementia. "We're worried about you."

Agnes shook her head, feeling the dry ends of her hair whip against her neck. "But why? I feel great."

"You haven't been yourself at all recently," Cindy said. She tapped both her feet against the floor looking very much like she wanted to get up and pace around the room but she remained seated. "I mean, the way you spoke to me last night was really odd. That's not you, Agnes."

"Because I said you couldn't come by?" That didn't seem

fair. Agnes tried to stand up but Esther's hands on her shoulders kept her seated.

"Well, that too," Cindy admitted. "But I'm talking about the rabbit. You told me yesterday that you thought he could read."

"And you keep claiming that he's helping you solve a murder," Esther added from behind the chair.

"Because he is," Agnes said. "And he can. Marshmallow's a genius. Let him go, Ashley, and he'll prove it."

The sixteen-year-old laughed uncomfortably. She scratched beneath the bunny's chin. "People think their pets are geniuses, but they're not."

"It also isn't logical," Margie cut in, voice firm but gentle. She moved forward so that she was barely perched on the edge of the couch. Stretching her arm, she rested a hand on Agnes' knee. "You're obviously suffering some sort of temporary delusion."

"And that rabbit is the cause of it all," Esther declared.

"It's true," Cindy said. "I'm sorry Agnes, but that bunny has got to go."

Chapter Twenty-Seven

MURDER BUNNY

I froze in my tracks. That was simply impossible. I'd been happy at Nigel's, but that time in my life had passed. Since then, I'd grown comfortable living in my new circumstance, here, in this vintage but warm Victorian house. Unreliable though Agnes could be, she loved and cared for me. I could tolerate her quite well.

It was a real shame that I'd caused her all this trouble. I sighed quietly to myself and felt some regret. I couldn't take back what I'd done that day with the red yarn on the ground. I couldn't put the toothpaste back in the tube, or stuff a carrot back into the ground. I'd disclosed everything. There was only one way forward.

Someone placed me in my cage. I pretended to be docile. Now was not the time for rebellion or huge gestures. I remained still, watching and listening.

Agnes was nearly hyperventilating. She didn't seem to handle stress very well.

"Oh sweetie," said Cindy.

But Agnes wasn't going to listen to them. She stood up, unsteady on her long thin legs, like a baby deer. She put a hand over her mouth and ran out of the room. I saw the bathroom door close behind her.

The others looked at one another. "I knew this was going to happen," said Cindy.

"Someone had to say it," said Margie, "and it may as well have been us."

"I know, I know."

"Just look at him," said Esther. All the faces turned and looked at me. "There's no way an animal like that could be smart enough to solve mysteries."

"Though, it's tempting to think—" Ashley began.

"—that pets are geniuses, thank you Ashley," interrupted her grandmother.

I remained stock still. I didn't dare to twitch a whisker. I felt that my entire existence hung by the thinnest of threads. I was walking on the knife's edge. Bunnies have a strong fight or flight mode, but I did neither. I just froze.

"After the medical examiner's report comes out," Margie said, "we'll see that Nigel died of natural causes. And maybe she'll give up all these silly stories she's telling herself."

"Maybe not," said Cindy.

"Why?" said Ashley.

"We all know her. Agnes has a quirky personality. This could be the next phase of her life."

"So you're saying that Agnes is losing her mind for real?" said Esther. "She's been a bit odd at work, but I just thought that's who she normally was."

"It's not impossible," answered Cindy. "I mean, she's living here alone in her grandmother's house, filled with her grandmother's furniture and clothes. It would drive me out of my mind too."

"So you're saying we should hold another intervention to get rid of her stuff and bring her back to normal," said Esther.

"What's she going to do in the Bake-Off tomorrow?" said Ashley. "Do you think she'll be okay to compete?"

"Dear, even at her best, Agnes wouldn't be ready to participate in a baking contest," Margie joked.

The women laughed, but I couldn't believe my floppy ears. They were supposed to be Agnes' friends. While I supposed they did care about her, the way they so callously dismissed her stories about a talking bunny offended me to my very core. For a moment, I thought about using my food pellets to spell out something unmentionable on the floor of my cage, which would put an immediate end to their dismissal of her, but I thought better of it. I had to control the disclosure very carefully: no rash or heated decisions. It's like the advice about writing down your anger in a letter and waiting twenty-four hours before sending it.

I would probably still be angry tomorrow, though. After all, they'd minimized and denigrated my own existence.

Agnes came out of the bathroom. "Agnes dear," said Margie, "come back over here. We love you and want nothing but the best for you."

Agnes came back into the room, nervous and tentative. "I don't want you to take the rabbit."

I exhaled, relieved. She was going to fight for me. Agnes was a real one. She'd jumped in the foxhole with me and wasn't going to let any soldiers drag me out.

The women all exchanged looks. I'm not expert on human body language, but they seemed to be communicating helplessness.

"I guess we can't stop you," said Esther, "but you shouldn't take it out of the house anymore."

"I agree," added Cindy.

"Just let the bunny be, right where he is," said Margie. "Is that acceptable?"

Agnes nodded. Her body language visibly relaxed. "So I guess that means you can all go now?"

"Of course," said Cindy. "I have things to do today anyways."

The four visitors stood up and took turns embracing Agnes on their way out the door. She closed it behind them. "Thank God," she said.

After the cars had pulled away, Agnes came over to my cage. "It's probably safer to leave you here anyways," she said. "I'll investigate Sandra Lee on my own. Let's compare notes when I come back, okay?"

I gave her a little flip to show I'd understood, that I was excited for her return. Human owners eat that kind of stuff up. I do it to humor them.

Agnes picked up her bag and walked over to the front door. It closed behind her. I was alone in the house.

It's been a long day, and I was growing very drowsy. We bunnies do need our naps. Before long, I'd passed out in my cage.

That's why I didn't hear the door open again. I didn't hear the heavy footsteps cross the floor. I didn't hear the man who unlocked my cage, I didn't wake up when he grabbed me roughly by the scruff of my neck, and I didn't feel him shove me into a canvas sack.

"Time to go, bunny," his voice said.

Chapter Twenty-Eight

AGNES

Agnes peeped out from behind a hydrangea bush. A pair of binoculars pressed rings around her eyes.

A little ways down the street, Sandra Swat emerged from her house. She wore a pair of jeans and a white blouse, her typical attire when working at her salon. The hair dresser held her phone to one ear while she hunted in her purse with the other. She pulled out her keys, unlocked her car, and climbed in.

Agnes held her breath as the engine revved. Finally, after an hour of waiting, the moment had arrived.

Once Sandra's car had disappeared from view, Agnes put her binoculars away and slipped out from behind the bush. She hurried to the hair dresser's property.

Sandra lived in a two-story house with cream-colored brick walls and a green roof. She'd inherited it from her ex-husband after a lengthy divorce battle. With the additional money she'd won in the settlement, Sandra Lee had converted half of the first floor into a hair salon.

Agnes tried the door. People in Warrenton seldom locked

their doors. They considered their town safe from the dangers that plagued bigger cities.

However, Sandra must have been more cautious because the door refused to budge, no matter how much Agnes pushed on it.

"Maybe this was a mistake," Agnes muttered to herself. The first sign of a problem, and she was ready to give it up.

What would Marshmallow think when she came home with no new information?

No! Agnes couldn't quit. Someone had murdered Nigel, and she'd promised to find out who. She couldn't do that if she didn't properly investigate.

Agnes crept around the side of the property. On the opposite side of the house to the salon, one of the windows had been left ajar. Perhaps, she could slip her hand through, push it open fully, and climb in that way.

However, when Agnes arrived at the window, she had a terrible crisis of conscience. She'd intended to walk into an unlocked salon. Whatever her intentions, forcing her way in through a window felt a lot like breaking and entering.

But she had to do something, Agnes reminded herself.

She slipped her hand through the window. Instead of attempting to force it open, however, she pushed a floral curtain aside, allowing her to see in.

Sandra's kitchen lay on the other side of the window. Orange lines stained the white countertops, and green leafy tops sprouted from the disposal in the sink. A red stand mixer stood in a kitchen island in the center. Beside it, a recipe book had been left open to a carrot cake recipe. Someone had scribbled over the page with a black pen. Each note had been crossed out several times.

"Caught you!" A hand slammed down on Agnes' shoulder.

Agnes gasped as someone spun her around.

It was Sandra Swat herself. The hairdresser's red-painted lips twisted in a scowl. "I knew you were up to something! Sneaking around with a pair of binoculars and hiding behind my neighbors' hedges."

"I'm sorry—"

"You look insane, Agnes. And even worse, your grand-mother would be ashamed."

Agnes couldn't believe it. This whole time, she'd thought she'd been doing some top-notch investigating, but Sandra had known she was there. The hairdresser must have driven off to trick Agnes and lure her out, then sneaked back on foot.

Now, the hairdresser's glare made Agnes' knees tremble and threaten to buckle beneath her.

"Let me guess," Sandra continued, still holding Agnes' shoulder. "You're trying to steal the recipe for my strawberry cheesecake, aren't you? Hah! The nerve!"

The accusation was so off base that it shook Agnes from her fright. She stepped out from beneath Sandra's grip and straightened, feeling a sudden steel to her spine.

"You're the thief!" Agnes pointed to the kitchen through the window. "There's no strawberry cheesecake! You're trying to steal Nigel's carrot cake recipe. Just what were you doing on the night of the announcement dinner?"

"I—who—what—excuse me?" Sandra sputtered for a moment. "What exactly are you suggesting?"

For once, Agnes decided to be blunt. "Someone broke into Nigel's home on the night of the Announcement Dinner. Was it you looking for his recipe?"

"That is absurd!" Sandra scoffed. "I'm not trying to *steal* Nigel's recipe. I'm trying to come up with a better one of my own. There's no glory in an empty win!"

"What do you mean?"

"Oh, honestly, Agnes, are you going to make me come out and say it?" Sandra sighed and sank against the wall beside her window. She opened her purse and pulled a compact mirror from her bag. She addressed the rest of her confession to her reflection. "Nigel would have won the Bake-Off again. I doubt you can do anything with his recipe. You haven't the skill. I tried his carrot cake at the fair. It was disgustingly delicious! But I don't want to mimic his. I want to make a better one." She closed the mirror. "So far I've had very little luck."

Sandra sounded so disappointed that Agnes felt a pang of sympathy. Perhaps the hair dresser wasn't the killer.

"Then, why didn't you go to the Announcement Dinner?" Agnes asked, stepping backward and almost tripping over an empty flower pot on the lawn.

"I did go," Sandra said.

Agnes crossed her arms and stared at the hair dresser. "I'm going to need a bit more than that."

"Oh, for Pete's sake, Agnes! You're not a detective," Sandra objected, but she opened her purse and pulled out her phone. It took a few seconds, but then she shoved it under Agnes' face.

On the screen was a picture of Sandra with an unimpressed-looking Josephine Charles. The background of the photograph showed the community hall on the night of the Announcement Dinner. Half-empty plates remained on the white tablecloths. One featured the leftover crust from a slice of blueberry pie.

If dessert had already been served and forgotten, then Sandra couldn't have left the dinner early.

"See? I was there," Sandra said, pulling the phone away and shoving it back into her purse. "Though I can't say I'm surprised you didn't see me. I was stuck comforting Marie for most of the night and never even had a chance to schmooze the judges. Josephine was the only one I found, and, let's be honest, there's no schmoozing that old hag."

Sandra went on complaining for a few more minutes, but Agnes was only half listening. The hair dresser had an alibi for the break-in, and her story about making her own recipe seemed believable.

That left only two people on Agnes' suspect list.

Chapter Twenty-Nine

AGNES

"We need to look into either Sebastian or Lilah next," Agnes announced as she pushed open the door. To her surprise, it had been unlocked. Strange. She could've sworn she'd used her key before leaving.

Agnes expected the bunny to come rushing. He was always ready to investigate. But there was no patter of little feet hopping across the hardwood floor.

"Marshmallow?" Agnes called, hurrying into the living room without dropping her bag.

Her initial thought was that he'd gotten stuck in his crate somehow. But the metal door swung open, no rabbit in sight.

Worry quickened Agnes' heart as she raced through the house. She dropped to her knees, searching under furniture for any sign of a fluffy white tail. But Marshmallow had vanished.

Agnes could think of only one person who would've taken him.

Cindy had been at the intervention. Cindy had said multiple times that her daughters wanted a pet bunny. And Cindy had a spare key for the house.

"Oh, the absolute nerve!" Agnes shouted to the empty room before rushing back to her car.

The drive to Cindy's house took about fifteen minutes. Agnes didn't speed, but she didn't extend the abundance of courtesy that she usually did either. When she had the right of way, she took it.

Agnes parked on the road outside her friend's house, jumped out, and marched to the door. She raised her hand to ring the bell, then reconsidered.

Cindy had never been very considerate with Agnes' space. What politeness was she owed in this instance?

Agnes pushed open the door, letting herself in. No permission asked.

Cindy's front door opened into a living area that had more toys than furniture. Dolls spilled out across a stained cream couch, and a small zoo of plastic animals spread out across the television stand. A collection of books, covers colored with crayons and pages crushed in a manner that made Agnes wince, sat on the coffee table.

Rebecca, the youngest of Cindy's daughters, leapt from one armchair to another. She almost slipped on a pair of dirty socks that someone had left on the cushions, but managed to catch herself.

"Oh no! Aunty Aggie!" Rebecca shouted as Agnes stepped off the welcome mat by the door. "The floor is lava! You just died!"

"It's okay. I have lava-destroying shoes," Agnes said, forcing a smile. "Can you get your mom for me, Rebecca?"

"Sure," the girl agreed. Then she leaned her head back and screeched at the top of her lungs, "Mom!"

Agnes covered her ears. Poor Marshmallow! He must be absolutely miserable in this den of chaos. The rabbit liked peace, quiet, and chamomile tea. Cindy would provide him none of those things!

"Rebecca, throw those socks in the laundry basket!" Cindy demanded, spotting her daughter before she saw Agnes by the door. At the sight of her, Cindy's eyebrows rose in obvious surprise.

"They're dad's socks," Rebecca argued. "And the lava will kill me, Mom!"

"Well, put them on and pretend they're part of the furniture," Cindy ordered.

Rebecca seemed to like that idea. She slipped her father's socks on her feet then skidded toward the kitchen, which had the laundry room attached. "Bye, Aunty Aggie! Sorry you died of lava when you were already sick!"

"I'm not sick!" Agnes shouted after the girl, but it was no use.

"What are you doing here, Aggie?" Cindy asked, making a half-hearted effort to tidy the dolls so that there was space to sit on the couch. "Not that I mind, but you almost never visit."

"I'm here for Marshmallow," Agnes said.

Cindy's brow furrowed and a pained look came over her face. She stopped tidying the dolls. "You're not still on about that rabbit, are you? Gosh, Agnes, you really should just let me take it. A bunny isn't a weird pet for an adult. I always thought Nigel was a bit—"

"You cannot have Marshmallow," Agnes said. Her voice was louder than she'd intended.

Cindy scoffed. "Well, you don't have to shout. I'm only looking out for you."

"No, you're not," Agnes insisted, marching toward her friend. "He's my rabbit, and you can't take him."

"Fine." Cindy chucked one of the dolls back onto the couch.

"So where is he?" Agnes demanded.

"Hopping around your house instead of being properly

crated, I assume," Cindy muttered. She grabbed a pair of dolls and pushed them toward Agnes. "Look, I don't want to fight about your rabbit. If you're going to stand here, help me clean up."

Agnes crossed her arms, making no move to take the dolls. "I know you have Marshmallow, Cindy."

"Excuse me?"

"He was missing when I went home. Who else would have taken him?"

Cindy dropped her arms, dolls dangling from their hair at her sides. She laughed. "Oh, this is rich. Agnes, you probably forgot to close the door, and he slipped out."

"I didn't!"

"Well, I certainly didn't steal him! And I can't believe you think I would," Cindy said. "We've been friends since we were five years old. I'm not going to steal your things!"

The anger that had been building in Agnes faltered at this statement. She'd known Cindy for almost her entire life. Did she really think that her friend would steal from her?

"I don't know," Agnes admitted, to herself as much as Cindy. "You keep saying that you want Marshmallow."

"I'd like that old collection of clothes your grandma left behind too, and some of those books that you refuse to lend me," Cindy argued. "But I've never just gone upstairs and helped myself to them, have I?"

"Certainly you use them when you're there," Agnes muttered, but her heart wasn't in the comment. Part of her did resent the way Cindy allowed her daughters to raid Agnes' house, but her friend's comfort with the place had never bothered her outside of that. And, for all Cindy's flaws, she always tried to be a good friend.

If she'd taken Marshmallow, she wouldn't lie about it. Sure, she might bulldoze over Agnes' feelings without listening, but Cindy would admit that she had the bunny and insist that she'd done it for Agnes' own good. In short, this would be a very different conversation.

Which meant only one thing: Cindy did not have Marshmallow.

"I'm not fighting with you because you're upset you lost your pet rabbit," Cindy snapped, beginning to gather the dolls again. "It's a good lesson about shutting your door properly."

"But I *did* shut it," Agnes said, running her hands through her hair. Perhaps her friend didn't see the seriousness of the situation. "Someone's bunny-napped Marshmallow!"

Cindy snorted. "Be serious, Aggie. No one's going to steal a rabbit."

"They might if they knew he was the only witness to a murder."

"Shh!" Cindy dropped all the dolls, letting them fall to the floor, as she hurried around the couch. She took Agnes by the shoulders. "Keep your voice down. I don't want the kids to hear how crazy you sound. They're already worried about you."

Agnes shook her head. She didn't understand why Cindy's kids should be worried about her. "Nigel was murdered, Cindy. I'm sure of it. And the killer must have snuck into my house looking for the carrot cake recipe. They probably stole Marshmallow so he couldn't give away their identity."

Cindy pressed her hand to Agnes' forehead. "I think the stress of the Bake-Off is getting to you. I'll drive you home. And we'll figure out how you're going to make a carrot cake on a stage in front of an audience without embarrassing yourself."

Chapter Thirty

AGNES

"This is Nigel's carrot cake recipe?" Cindy held up the piece of paper in disbelief.

Written in Delores Brooms' small cursive scrawl were instructions for how to bake a carrot cake. Agnes had found it in the large folder where her grandmother had stored all of her recipes. She was no expert, but it seemed like an ordinary recipe. Now she'd decided to pass it off as the dead man's ultra secret prized recipe.

"Nigel told me that he'd gotten the recipe from my grandmother before he died," Agnes lied, pulling a bag of flour from her basket of ingredients.

She was back in her grandmother's kitchen, but instead of the furry investigative partner she wanted, Agnes found herself with an overenthusiastic assistant baker. Finding Marshmallow and solving Nigel's murder should have been Agnes' top priority. However, Cindy insisted that Agnes focus on the Bake-Off. Helping Agnes prepare would also get her obsessive mind off the missing bunny.

"Delores was a good baker," Cindy admitted, slowly coming around to the idea. "So have you practiced making it yet?" She looked around the kitchen as though hoping to try a slice.

"Not yet," Agnes admitted.

"Seriously? Aggie, the contest is tomorrow! I know winning is a long shot, but you ought to at least be able to make something edible," Cindy said. She moved around the kitchen, pulling ingredients from the shelves.

Under different circumstances, Agnes would be inclined to agree. She'd intended to practice baking this afternoon. But with Marshmallow missing, things had changed.

Agnes started to explain, "I really need to find—"

"Your rabbit, I know," Cindy cut her off with a sigh. She stopped searching for the ingredients long enough to give Agnes a sympathetic smile. "But think about it. If that bunny is really as smart as you say, then he might've hopped out on his own and be coming back to you right now. Don't you think?"

Could Marshmallow have decided to investigate the murder on his own?

Agnes tilted her head as she considered. "It's not impossible."

"Exactly!" Cindy grinned at her. "So let's practice baking while we wait."

Cindy set about measuring flour and sugar, while Agnes took charge of vegetables and nuts. There were twelve carrots in total. Agnes had no idea how many she'd need to grate in order to get three cups, but she wouldn't have time to visit the store before the Bake-Off tomorrow. She couldn't risk wasting carrots in her practice cake, so she decided to substitute with other orange vegetables: pumpkin, sweet potato, and orange peppers all mixed into three cups. It looked similar enough to grated carrots if you squinted. Peanuts made a believable replacement for pecans too.

Agnes ground the nuts in a food processor before adding

them and the vegetable bits to the cake batter. She mixed the batter with a spoon, poured it into the cake pans Cindy had prepared, and stuck everything into the oven.

Once the kitchen had been cleaned, the cake still had a while in the oven. Cindy suggested retreating to the living room. Agnes complied. She needed to search for Marshmallow, but she couldn't leave the oven on either.

The two women sat in the armchairs with cups of tea. Cindy complained about Scott, and Agnes pretended to listen.

A large window showed the garden outside. Hedges surrounded the property, as was customary in Warrenton, but the yard also boasted a seventy-year-old oak tree. Delores herself had planted the acorn as a girl.

Agnes stared out the window, mind drifting to Nigel's murder as Cindy spoke. If the killer had bunny-napped Marshmallow, what were they planning to do to him?

A face peeped out from behind the oak's trunk. The sight crashed Agnes back to the present.

"There's someone on the lawn!" Agnes declared, leaping up.

"Who is it?" Cindy spun in her chair, but the person had ducked behind the tree again.

"I'll be back in a minute," Agnes said, hurrying from the living room without stopping to explain. If someone was skulking around her house, there was a good chance it was the killer. Perhaps they'd snuck in earlier looking for clues about the carrot cake recipe, and discovered Marshmallow instead. They might've taken the bunny hostage and be planning to leave a ransom note for Agnes now.

She grabbed a knife from the dishwasher, which had yet to be turned on. It was the same knife she'd used to cut vegetables. Warrenton was considered a safe town, but Agnes wasn't taking any chances.

Her heart pounded as she rounded the corner of the house and stepped into the large yard. She felt certain she was about to confront the killer.

"Agh! What are you doing?" a man's voice shouted.

Agnes' head spun toward the house. Pressed against the wall was none other than Sebastian Monroe, her current prime suspect. He wore a dark green shirt and camel-colored trousers that he'd rolled up at the ankle, showing his white socks. He held his palms up in a show of surrender.

"What?"

"I asked what you're doing with that knife?" Sebastian demanded. His voice held its usual thinly veiled contempt, but his face paled at the sight of the weapon.

Agnes kept the knife before her as she marched forward. "What are you doing creeping around my house?"

"Coming to speak to you, of course," Sebastian said. He clicked his tongue and pointed to the knife with a look of distaste. "It's covered with potato peels. You do know it's not designed for peeling vegetables, don't you?"

Agnes wiped the skins off the blade. "What could you possibly have to speak with me about?"

"The Bake-Off, of course," Sebastian said as though it were the most obvious thing in the world. "Aren't you going to invite me in so we can discuss it like civilized people?"

Agnes considered it. She'd had one encounter with a suspect in a garden already for the day, but allowing Sebastian into the kitchen seemed too risky. Even if he wasn't the killer, he didn't need to sneak around the side of the house to find Agnes. He was clearly hoping to find the carrot cake recipe.

"We can go onto the patio," Agnes offered. She tapped on the living room window as they walked passed, being certain to get Cindy's attention. If something happened, Agnes wanted to make sure someone knew that Sebastian had been there.

The patio furniture got significantly less wear than the rest. Agnes had never been much of an outdoor person. However, an overhanging ceiling sheltered the plastic chairs and metallic table from the worst of the elements. Even without use, they remained in good condition.

Sebastian eyed the seats as though they might transform into snakes and attack at any moment. "You really should come around and look at my catalog. I can get an excellent set of outdoor furniture, if you give me the word."

"You wanted to discuss the Bake-Off," Agnes reminded him.

"That I did," Sebastian admitted. He took a seat, grimacing and shifting as though the furniture pained him. This struck Agnes as unnecessarily silly given that the chairs each had a pair of floral cushions. "I've come to offer an alliance."

Agnes' eyebrows rose. She waited for Sebastian to mention Marshmallow in his speech that followed.

"We compete in the Bake-Off as a team," Sebastian suggested. "It's the only chance you have at winning. I'll do all the work of course. The only thing you need to provide is Nigel's recipe."

How odd, Agnes thought. *If he wants to trade the recipe for Marshmallow, then why doesn't he come out and offer?*

Aloud, Agnes said, "I didn't know you could work in teams for the Bake-Off."

"It's not common, but it's permitted—if one of the bakers can set aside their ego," Sebastian assured her with a haughty sniff. He crossed his arms and turned his nose into the air. "Nigel never could. I suggested teamwork to him once and he nearly laughed my head off. Said he didn't need me for anything. Hah! Nigel might've been talented when it came to flavor, but his decorating skills were ghastly. Always tried to distract with ridiculous toppers, as though sticking some old thing on to a cake will hide the uneven piping. I honestly thought he'd made a wedding cake at the fair until he corrected me. Told me it was the best carrot cake in existence, claimed there was a secret ingredient in the icing. Of course, he refused to give me a taste."

Agnes frowned. Several parts of Sebastian's story struck her as odd, but she couldn't think what reason he'd have to lie about them.

'Was it common for Nigel to refuse to give potential competitors a slice?" Agnes asked, still holding the knife toward the man in her patio chair. She feared if she lowered it, she might not lose the courage to raise it again.

"I don't know about the others, but he'd never share with me. My palette is far too sensitive. Nigel knew I'd figure out the ingredients from the flavor alone."

"Bet you'd have liked to swipe a bit of icing off the top of the cake," Agnes guessed.

"I suppose, but if you have the recipe now, I can—what is that smell?" Sebastian's nose wrinkled, and he stood. "Are you roasting vegetables?"

"I'm baking a cake," Agnes corrected.

Sebastian inhaled again, then he burst out laughing. "Oh that is rich! You really had me for a moment." He paused, looking at her expression. "You're joking, right?"

"I'm not," Agnes insisted. "I'm practicing for tomorrow."

Sebastian's eyebrows rose. "You're trying to tell me that you used Nigel's secret recipe and ended up with a cake that smells like that? It's like vegetable soup!"

Agnes sighed. "If you're going to be rude, you can leave."

Sebastian rose from his chair. "You haven't got Nigel's recipe. And you can forget what I said about teaming up. I'll let the whole town see you for the liar you are in the Bake-Off tomorrow, Agnes."

He walked to the edge of the patio, then turned back. For

a moment, Agnes thought he was going to say something about Marshmallow.

Instead, Sebastian gave her a dark smile. "Usually, I don't wish my competitors luck," he informed her. "But I'll make an exception in your case. Because Lord knows, you're going to need it."

Chapter Thirty-One

MURDER BUNNY

I awoke with a start and found myself in a completely dark sack. I knew it was a sack because the burlap was rubbing against my nose, chafing it. Also, my legs had somehow gotten over my head and had both gone completely asleep. I twisted myself around until they were back underneath me, and waited for the pins and needles to begin.

They did. It was awful and I fought the urge to whimper. I just gritted my teeth and waited for it to pass. When it did, I took stock of my situation.

I'd been placed on a hard surface. I could feel it beneath me. There was no light entering the sack, which meant either that the burlap was very thick or that I was in a dark place. Maybe it was nighttime. I had no idea how much time had passed since they'd stolen me.

It's an indignity. We bunnies don't get any respect. We need to stand up for ourselves more often.

Meanwhile, in order to stand up like a free animal again, I would need to escape from this sack. At first, I didn't know how exactly to accomplish that. I couldn't locate the opening, which was surely cinched tightly anyways.

Then I felt a thin string of burlap tickle my cheek. It was a loose thread. I grabbed it with my teeth and began to yank. It pulled easily, so I kept following it. Soon the thread had unspooled once around the entire sack. I continued pulling it out, my head going in circles. It was starting to hurt my neck.

The more I pulled, the more a narrow sliver of white light began to show through the sack. I grew excited. I realized that pulling the thread to escape would take hours, and that God had blessed me with two very strong teeth capable of chomping and chewing.

So I began to chew on the burlap.

I don't recommend it. Burlap tastes terrible. I much prefer the cognac that I had been fond of sipping from Nigel's snifter after he fell asleep late at night.

But at last I'd gnawed a sizable little hole in the sack, enough to wriggle my nose and eyes through.

I was in a dingy kitchen. I'd been placed on the floor, surrounded by piles of old newspapers. It was filled with dirty dishes, empty oil cans, and broken cabinetry. On the table above, I could see an ashtray overflowing with cigarette butts. There was nothing feminine or even pleasant about this one.

I hate to say it, but this was definitely a man's house. And not any man, but an untidy, uncivilized one.

Then I heard the voices outside the house. They were muffled and indistinct, but they were definitely male. My instincts had been dead on.

I pulled my face back into the sack, but kept the hole open enough to see what was happening.

The front door opened, and a pair of boots clomped into the house. They were followed by a pair of softer shoes. I couldn't see them but I could certainly hear them.

"God, this place is filthy," said one of the men.

"Well, I like it the way it is," said the other. "It's comfortable, I know where everything is. Besides, we can't all live in a beautiful place."

"All right, let's do what we came here to do," said the first.

"Okay—I left the little jerk over here."

The boots came towards me. I shrank back and my ears laid flat against my head. This was my worst nightmare.

Then I felt hands lifting me up in the sack, and I knew things were about to get much worse.

Chapter Thirty-Two

AGNES

Agnes forced a forkful of her own carrot cake down her throat. She lifted her eyeballs to the ceiling, thinking.

The attempt had proven to be unique. This might have been because it contained no carrots and could be considered cake only in the loosest sense. The texture succeeded in being both chewy and underbaked depending on the portion tested. Despite the sugar that Agnes had added to the batter, the sweet peppers and squash gave it a savory texture. But it wasn't inedible.

Cindy, meanwhile, had dumped it into the garbage.

"You can't serve that to the judges," Cindy said, taking a large drink of water. She swished it around her mouth before spitting into the sink. "They'll think you're plotting to kill them."

"I assure you, I'm not the murderer," Agnes muttered, without looking up. She sat at the kitchen table, flipping through the notes she'd made with Marshmallow. Since Sebastian had left, Agnes had been replaying the conversation in her mind. It was obvious that the furniture salesman was desperate to get his hands on Nigel's recipe. Was he desperate enough to kill for it?

And there was something else he'd said that didn't make sense—

"What are you doing? There's no time to read!" Cindy said, interrupting Agnes' thoughts. "You've got to keep practicing. Where are the carrots? I'll grate them for you this time."

"I can't focus on baking right now," Agnes objected, shaking her head. "I have to find Marshmallow!"

"Well, he's not in that book," Cindy snapped.

No, he was with Nigel's killer. Solving the case might be Agnes' only chance at saving him.

"I'm sorry, Aggie," Cindy said, taking a seat beside Agnes with a sigh. "Let's make a deal. We'll put up missing rabbit posters, and then we'll keep practicing. After all, Marshmallow wouldn't want you to embarrass yourself on stage tomorrow."

It didn't escape Agnes' notice that her friend was using the same tone that she did when bargaining with her daughters. But posters couldn't hurt. It was a long shot, but there was always the possibility of someone having spotted their neighbor carrying a white rabbit into their house.

So Agnes agreed to her friend's plan. Over the next few hours, they designed a poster, printed a hundred copies to distribute around Warrenton, and then split up in order to "divide and conquer", in Cindy's words. Agnes thought it was a chance to finally do something useful.

The posters had to be placed close to the houses and frequent haunts of the potential suspects. Agnes listed locations to herself as she carried the posters toward the front door: the Batter Chatter, the clinic where Lilah Dorchester worked, Sebastian's apartment and store.

Perhaps Agnes should take the opportunity to peek

through the furniture salesman's windows as well. There, she might find Marshmallow locked in a cage, and solve everything in a matter of seconds.

However, the moment Agnes stepped outside, she spotted something that forced her to put this plan on hold.

Across the street, Nigel's front door swung open. Someone was in his house.

She knew it had to be the killer. They'd come back to search for the carrot cake recipe a second time.

Agnes' immediate suspicion, of course, was that it was Sebastian. But she wanted evidence. So, instead of climbing into her car, Agnes pulled her phone from her purse and crept across the street. Her heart pounded, anxiety racing through her. But there was a sense of excitement to it as well. Agnes was finally going to catch a criminal.

Having learned from her run-in earlier with Sandra Swat, Agnes didn't rush straight to the window. Instead, she ducked behind a large hedge before the front door. Hidden among the leaves, she readied her phone's camera.

Footsteps sounded from within. She heard a man's voice. A shadow moved into the living room, partially visible through the open door.

Agnes started recording. She'd get a video of Sebastian leaving the house. That should be enough evidence to convince the police to take a closer look at the furniture salesman.

The figure within drew closer to the door and came into view on her camera. But it wasn't Sebastian.

"Evan!" Agnes exclaimed from the bush, almost dropping her camera as the young policeman stepped outside. "What are you doing in Nigel's house?"

"Aggie?" The young officer shielded his eyes from the sun with his hand and leaned forward to study her. "I'm the one who should be asking questions. Why are you hiding in a bush?"

Agnes brushed the leaves off her arms as she stepped out. "I thought the person who'd broken in the other night had returned. I was planning to record them and send the video to you."

"That's brave of you! Are you still the same Agnes Brooms that used to make me check under the bed for monsters?" Evan said. His voice had a cheerful laugh.

Agnes smiled, though she wasn't certain if the young officer was teasing her or being genuine in his compliment. Hiding in a bush was seldom lauded as a mark of bravery.

Evan also hadn't answered her question. Given his uniform, it appeared he was at Nigel's house in an official capacity.

"Are you still investigating the break-in?" Agnes guessed.

The bright smile fell from Evan's face as his expression turned nervous. He tugged at the collar of his shirt. "Not exactly. Listen, Aggie, if we're going to discuss this, we'd best do it in private. Come inside."

Agnes followed Evan without thinking. She had no reason to be suspicious of the boy. She'd known him since he was a baby.

Yet, as she followed him through the cozy living area, full of blankets, large chairs, and old-fashioned china cabinets, something struck Agnes as off.

"Where's your partner, Evan?" Agnes asked. The Warrenton sheriff's department could be lax, but she'd never seen a policeman operate alone. "And why isn't there a police car parked outside the property?"

"Because I'd prefer that no one know that I'm here," Evan admitted. "I'm not officially on the case."

He stopped in the center of the massive kitchen, sleek and modern, twice the size of the living and dining area combined. Two ovens had been installed, one on top the other amid the cabinetry. Red trimmed appliances gleamed atop the black counter tops with a stand-mixer in a place of pride. Glass doors on the cupboards showed the many mixing bowls and measuring implements within.

Evan continued in a low voice, "I shouldn't be telling you this, Aggie, but you were right. The coroner's report came back yesterday. Someone poisoned Nigel."

The officer paused, looking at Agnes as though he expected a response to this. Maybe shock, maybe horror, maybe a touch of hysteria that a murderer was nearby.

Agnes felt none of this. Nor did she feel the relief that she'd expected she might when she got confirmation that Nigel had been murdered. After all, it was evidence that she wasn't inventing stories the way her friends thought. However, the officer's statement affected Agnes the same way that it would have had he informed her that the sky was blue. That confounded her more than anything else.

Since when have I been so certain about myself?

"The Sheriff wants to label it a suicide and brush the whole thing under the rug."

"It definitely wasn't," Agnes said quickly.

"I agree," Evan continued in a whisper, "But Sheriff Mogg swears there are no killers in Warrenton. If it was murder, he reckons it must've been some deranged out-of-towner who'll have skipped off after the fair. He thinks if we announce an investigation and start looking into things, people will get spooked, and the mayor will insist we make an arrest. The wrong person is liable to end up in jail."

"Surely not, if you all do your jobs right!"

"I'm only relaying the Sheriff's concerns." Evan raised his hands to placate her. "I actually agree with you. That's why I came here. I thought I might find a clue as to why someone might kill Nigel."

"For his carrot cake recipe, of course. Why else?" Agnes paused, studying the kitchen anew. It wasn't just clean and modern, but perfectly arranged. "Did you all tidy up after the break-in?"

Evan shook his head no. "The kitchen wasn't touched. Nothing in this house was. It was the antique store that got ransacked. A group of teenage boys looking for stuff to pawn for a quick buck. One of them approached Mr. Thornton trying to sell him a clock."

Agnes chewed the skin on her thumb, considering this new information. Brandon Dorchester had left the Announcement Dinner early. Earlier this year, he'd gotten into trouble for shoplifting and graffiting several park benches. Breaking into Nigel's store sounded like just the sort of thing he and his friends would get into.

That meant that Agnes had been operating with faulty information. She'd assumed the killer couldn't have been at the Announcement Dinner, and had narrowed down her suspects in that way. But if the break-in wasn't connected to Nigel's murder, the list of suspects needed to be expanded again.

Chapter Thirty-Three

AGNES

Beep. Beep. Beep!

Her grandmother's old alarm clock screeched at Agnes the next morning. She turned to slap the button that would snooze it, then caught sight of the time. It was after nine o'clock.

She had to be at the Bake-Off in less than an hour!

Agnes flew out of bed, grabbed a dress from her cupboard, and wriggled out of her nightgown and into it as she hurried to the bathroom. The face that stared back at her in the mirror appeared haunted. Two dark half-moons puffed up beneath her eyes, and her hair poofed like she'd been shocked by static electricity.

In a desperate attempt to appear less ghoulish, she flattened her hair with water and tied it tight behind her. Then, she scrubbed her face, but no amount of soap could wipe away the evidence of her lack of sleep.

Yesterday, after leaving Nigel's house, Agnes had put up the missing bunny posters as planned. She'd even gone into Sebastian's store and searched for hints of white fur. But neither of his two employees could tell her anything about a rabbit. After an annoyed Cindy had called her, Agnes had been forced to return to her house. She'd managed to bake something edible, though still technically not *carrot* cake since she kept omitting that key ingredient. But Cindy said the judges wouldn't throw up if she served it.

Personally, that was good enough for Agnes. She didn't need to win the contest; she wanted to solve the murder. The Bake-Off would be her best chance. All of her suspects would be gathered in one place. She'd have no better chance to investigate.

Agnes had tossed and turned in bed, worrying about Marshmallow and struggling to think how best to proceed. The bunny would have known. He would have come up with just the right trap to catch the killer. She could have distracted the other contestants while he investigated their bags for clues. But there was no sense thinking of those possibilities because Marshmallow wouldn't be there to help. Agnes would need to solve things on her own.

But since Marshmallow's disappearance, Agnes feared she'd somehow gotten further away from the solution. Any one of the competitors might have killed Nigel. And yet, a curious inconsistency nagged at her mind.

"Focus, Agnes," she instructed her reflection, splashing water on her face once more.

She had to get to the Bake-Off on time. Arriving late would mean automatic disqualification. Then she'd lose her chance to investigate at all.

Agnes hurried from the bathroom and down the steps. She needed to grab her ingredients, head to the car, and—

"Morning, Aggie! What's for breakfast?"

Agnes jumped at the sound of a man's voice coming from her kitchen. Terror shot through her for a split second before her uncle's round, unshaven face appeared through the doorway.

"Didn't I tell you I was going to call the police next time you showed up uninvited, Uncle Curtis?" Agnes said, storming into the kitchen. She opened the fridge and grabbed the bag of ingredients that she'd put together the night before. Then she paused.

Does this bag feel lighter?

Uncle Curtis laughed. "Oh come on. I just came to borrow some food. Hardly a crime."

"Yes, it is. It's stealing," Agnes informed him. She opened the bag. It was empty. "What have you done with my ingredients, Uncle Curtis?"

"Unpacked them for you," he said, cutting himself a slice of the cake Agnes had successfully baked yesterday. "No need to thank me. Though it was rather lazy of you not to bother when you got back from the store."

"Those are my ingredients! I need them for the Bake-Off." Agnes hunted through the fridge, scrambling to remember everything that had been in the bag. Cindy had been the one who'd gotten it ready. Agnes barely remembered.

"You're competing in the Bake-Off?" Uncle Curtis bellowed with laughter. "Now that I have to see!"

"Thanks for the vote of support," Agnes muttered, pulling cream cheese, butter, and eggs out of the fridge and shoving them into her bag. What else was she missing?

Carrots.

Agnes opened the drawers at the bottom of her fridge. They'd been emptied.

"Did you take all my vegetables?" Agnes slammed the fridge and spun to face her uncle.

He held a large slice of cake in a paper towel on his hand, eating it without regard for cutlery or dishware. Crumbs fell onto his protruding stomach. Peeking out on the kitchen table behind him was the corner of an old wicker basket, which had previously belonged to Agnes' grandmother. Her uncle must have accidentally borrowed that as well.

"I left the garlic and onion," Uncle Curtis said, as though this somehow exonerated him.

Agnes didn't have time to yell at him. She opened the basket and rummaged through a head of lettuce, three tomatoes, and several green peppers to find the carrots buried below. Her uncle must have finally been taking his doctor's advice about dieting.

Uncle Curtis shoved the last of her cake into his mouth and spoke while he chewed. "Ya know, this isn't disgusting. A bit stale, but baked goods do have a short shelf life."

"I made it last night," Agnes informed him. She added the carrots to her bag, then searched quickly for additional ingredients: flour, sugar, vanilla essence.

"Last night?" Uncle Curtis said, spitting crumbs. "It's dry as a bag of sand!"

"You just said you liked it," Agnes complained.

Her uncle slapped Agnes on the back with such force that she lost her footing and stumbled into the counter. "Aggie, the judges are going to roast you alive. It's going to be like a comedy show. Wowee!"

"Get out of my house, Uncle Curtis," Agnes snapped, shouldering her bag and rushing out the door. She saw no signs of him following by the time she'd reached her car.

But this isn't his fault. It's mine.

Agnes knew how her uncle was. She couldn't expect him to change. If she wanted him to stop barging into her home, she needed to use force to stop him.

Sitting behind the wheel of her car, Agnes pulled out her phone, looked up a number, and dialed.

A woman's voice answered on the other end. "Safe Solutions Locksmithing Company, how can I assist you?"

Chapter Thirty-Four

AGNES

Agnes made it to her destination with five minutes to spare. However, Monica Duncan, who'd been assigned the task of checking everyone in, acted as though Agnes were hours late.

Monica's heels clicked across the parking lot as she led Agnes to the backdoor of a large cylindrical glass building. "Have you been on the stage of the Puck before?"

Goodfellow Theatre, nicknamed the Puck by locals, was considered by many to be the crown jewel of Warrenton. The theatre had been funded in large part by Josephine Charles and her late husband. Every performance took place on its stage from children's ballet recitals to blues concerts by visiting musicians.

"No—well, yes, I mean, sort of," Agnes offered lamely as she walked through the back entrance of the theater. "I went on stage on a field trip once, but I've never performed on it."

Monica offered Agnes curt bits of advice as they wound through the backstage corridors. "Don't look directly at the overhead lights, or you'll look more out of it than usual. Keep to your own workspace. Move quickly. This isn't a home kitchen. You can't spend hours weighing the flour to get the perfect hundred grams."

Agnes' brow furrowed. "Am I supposed to be weighing flour?"

Monica scoffed in response and led her onstage. The Puck's stage had been transformed into a massive kitchen like what one might find on a television cooking show. Five work stations had been set up in the loose shape of an *M,* ensuring each contestant could be seen by the many rows of seats rising in the auditorium. Each station featured a black stove-top, shiny white counters, and a small fridge. Six ovens stacked in two rows of three gleamed at the back of the stage.

"I put you in the back," Monica said, moving toward the work station furthest from where they'd entered, her heels click-clacking on the floor of the stage. She gave Agnes a quick overview of the workstation, the appliances, and locations of the shared pots, pans, and trays for contestants.

"So that's everything. If you need anything else, you'll have to have someone bring it over, or just make do without."

Agnes noticed the judges in the back of the room, getting directions from a man with a video camera. Only Dr. Michaels appeared to be listening. Tobias Thornton was checking his watch, and Josephine Charles, who judged the contest every year, wasn't even pretending. She faced away from the man, tapping her fingers impatiently and studying the stage. Her eyes narrowed at Agnes, as if in judgment.

Or perhaps that disapproval was only in Agnes' mind. She'd had very little interaction with the wealthy widow. There was no reason for Josephine to dislike her.

Then she led her back through the twisting corridors backstage and into the dressing room where the other contestants waited.

Sandra sat before a mirror, arguing with a stylist attempting to flat iron her bob. Margie and Lilah sat on a long couch near the back. Both women already had bright red makeup on their cheeks and lips, and their hair had been pinned onto their heads. They appeared to be engaged in conversation, though Lilah was doing most of the talking. Sebastian cracked his knuckles in the corner beside them, facing the wall and bouncing on his toes, as though preparing for a boxing match instead of a bake-off. None of their clothes or shoes showed any hint of white fur.

Agnes waved awkwardly in greeting. Margie gave her a warm smile, Lilah offered a curt nod, and Sandra snorted.

Sebastian gasped. "Goodness, what happened to you? It looks like someone's punched both your eyes."

Agnes wanted to sweep her hair over her face, sink into the floor, and hope they all forgot she'd ever been there. But if she wanted to solve Nigel's murder and recover Marshmallow, she'd need to control his conversation.

With a deep breath, Agnes summoned her most convincing voice. "I stayed up practicing for the contest. Nigel's recipe isn't easy to follow, but I think I've finally got it."

The lie was lost as Monica barked orders to the stylist and shoved Agnes into the available chair. The young stylist rushed from Sandra to attend to the newcomer. For a moment, the only sound was the swish of the makeup brush across the powdered foundation and over Agnes' face.

"I have to go, everybody," said Monica, looking at a message on her phone. "One hour until showtime." She marched out of the room, and the door closed behind her. The other four contestants leaned closer the moment Monica had vanished.

"What I smelled yesterday was a disaster," Sebastian whispered, eyes narrowing in suspicion. "Agnes, it was nothing like one of Nigel's recipes."

"I was trying to go off memory," Agnes said. "But I forgot almost everything. I'm so scatterbrained. I'm just going to follow Nigel's exact instructions written down today."

She produced her grandmother's recipe from her pocket and waved it in the air. She'd written it down on a pair of index cards in her own handwriting.

Sandra looked at her with rage. "Are you mad? We don't bring our recipes to the Bake-Off! Let alone one of Nigel's!"

"Agnes, you must be very careful to hide that," Margie instructed. "How did you get that? Nigel didn't sell you his recipe."

"No, but someone else did," Agnes said, inhaling deeply. She didn't think she'd ever told so many lies in her life, but it couldn't be helped. "I purchased an antique box from Brandon Dorchester and found several of Nigel's recipes within."

Sandra's eyes widened. "You didn't mention that at the Batter Chatter."

"You didn't need to know. Now you do."

At the mention of her son, all eyes turned to Lilah.

"Pah!" She slapped her hand on the couch, and her large frame wobbled beneath her sunflower yellow dress. "You sound like Sheriff Mogg now. My Brandon had nothing to do with any robbery."

"I caught him trying to slip a vase into his jacket and out of my store two weeks ago," Sebastian muttered wryly. Then, he turned to Agnes. "If it's really Nigel's recipe, I'll give you double what you paid for it."

"Not to bake today!" Sandra Lee exclaimed, dropping the flat-iron she'd taken control of and spinning in her seat. "That's against the rules. You can't change your entry now."

"I could," Sebastian objected. "The qualifiers never happened. This is essentially a free for all."

"It would be rather underhanded," Margie said.

"This is all nonsense," Lilah continued. "Absolute nonsense! I'm telling you, Brandon didn't steal any recipe box for her to buy. He spent that night shooting fireworks by the creek with his friends."

Agnes listened to the argument that ensued, praying for a clue in the chaos as the stylist swished brushes over her eyelids and sprayed her hair.

Then Monica shoved the door open and began barking orders. Agnes found herself pulled from her chair before she could catch more than a glimpse of herself in the mirror. Her lips and cheeks looked garishly red, and her hair had stiffened into a helmet of unnatural waves. Still, it was probably an improvement.

———

The contestants marched in single file onto the stage and practiced where they were to stand during the filming. Then, they were ordered off again as a flood of people entered the theatre and took their seats. Agnes spotted Cindy and her daughters among them.

"Line up," Monica ordered, shoving the contestants into a line. "Wait for your cue. Remember, stop in the center. Smile, wave, and walk to your station."

Sebastian stood fourth in line, just in front of Agnes. The lifts in his shoes brought him to her height. He flexed his hands, rolled his shoulders, and muttered under his breath, "Red leather, yellow leather, red leather, yellow leather."

The inconsistency that had haunted Agnes last night sprang into her mind again. She leaned forward and tapped

Sebastian's shoulder. He jumped in shock, but Agnes didn't waste time with an apology.

"Why did you think Nigel had made a wedding cake when you saw it at the fair?" she asked.

"Are you trying to throw me off my game before we go on stage?" Sebastian hissed. "I don't want to think about Nigel's cake!"

Agnes pressed further, ignoring his objection. "Did it have a topper?"

"Of course! It was some hideous old church or something. That's why I thought it was a wedding cake. But it's too late to think about how you want to decorate your cake now."

On that point, Sebastian was correct. The mayor was already on stage, welcoming the spectators both in-person and watching on television. The Bake-Off was about to begin!

Chapter Thirty-Five

MURDER BUNNY

It is a unique feeling of shame when the only item of clothing you own is ripped off your body.

Ladies, imagine wearing a single one-piece swimsuit that gets sliced in half by a trickster with a pocketknife, and you have to clutch your arms over your unmentionables while running for shelter. Gentlemen, imagine someone ten times your size reaching into your bathroom and yanking the tighty-whities right off your body, leaving you jaybird naked.

That second scenario is what happened to me. The hands that had reached into the bag had unclasped the collar that had always hung around my neck. Then they removed it. I couldn't believe it. I'd felt like that collar had become a part of me. They may as well have removed my pancreas.

Then the hands disappeared and the boots did too. The front door closed. I was alone. So I hopped out of the bag and leapt onto the floor and frolicked and gamboled through the house, totally nude. I honestly don't know what got into me. I suddenly knew why those silly animals, what do you call them? Ah yes—*dogs*—I knew why they got the zoomies. I was getting them too.

I was sure of one thing: I'd been kidnapped for that carrot cake recipe. Don't ask me how or why. It was something that I just knew in my little bunny heart.

After an hour, the front door opened, and the boots came back into the house. I scurried back into the kitchen and leapt into my sack and peered out.

"Bunny bunny bunny," said the man's voice.

When he came around the corner, I recognized his face. It was Uncle Curtis.

Uncle Curtis had kidnapped me.

He was carrying a cardboard box, which he placed on the floor. Then he went to the refrigerator and removed some vegetables and chopped them up.

"Chop chop chop, chop all day, gonna give bunny some food, right where he lay," Uncle Curtis said. It was a freeform scat. He was having fun.

Then he turned and dumped the vegetables into the cardboard box. "This is going to be your new home, bunny. Right inside a comfortable piece of cardboard." He gave a stupid laugh. Then he reached into the sack and grabbed me by my scruff and lifted me into the air.

"Lemme tell you something, Marshmallow. That's what she calls you, right?" I nodded. "Yeah, I'm not a bad guy. I'm not good, but I'm not bad either. In fact, I like you. I want you to live. I want you to be comfortable. That's why I got you this new house."

He lowered me into the box. I found myself sitting on a bed of vegetables. This was highly embarrassing. It is a terrible thing to be forced to sit on a pile of one's own food.

Uncle Curtis wagged a finger at me. "You be good. I'll be right back. I've got a baking competition to attend."

Then he closed the flaps on the top of the box. I was left in darkness, like some kind of underground cave troll sitting on his creepy little bed of worthless treasure, sucking down pale fish with no eyeballs and going slowly insane.

Then I remembered something. Had he said he was going to a baking competition? If so, it had to be the Bake-Off. And boy did I ever need to get to that competition.

His boots walked off; I heard him enter the bathroom. There was no time to waste: I immediately began chewing through the cardboard. It was easy. Uncle Curtis had no idea just how strong my two front chompers were. Most people don't. We bunnies have some serious teeth.

Soon there was a hole in the cardboard. The toilet flushed and the door opened. Uncle Curtis walked the rest of the way to the front door.

I squealed, then squeezed through the hole in the box and galloped across the floor. He was halfway out the door when I slipped out with him, as quiet as an Anglican's bedroom. I ducked into a hedge as he turned and locked his door.

Then he ran to his truck and slipped behind the wheel. I quickly ran to the back, leapt onto the bumper ledge, then hopped up and over the gate and into the bed.

The truck rumbled to life and began to pull into the street. I laid flat, feeling the vehicle beneath me.

I was headed to the Bake-Off.

Chapter Thirty-Six

AGNES

Somehow, in the midst of solving a murder, Agnes had forgotten her crippling stage fright.

It hit her full force the moment she stepped out of the wings. Bright lights blinded her, forcing Agnes to gape and blink like a fish.

Strangers stared at her from the audience. As she lowered her gaze from the lights, she recognized some familiar faces. Ashley smiled at her, sitting near the front with friends. Further to the back, Esther looked nervous. In the middle of the crowd, Cindy and her daughters shouted and waved.

Agnes couldn't wave back. Her limbs had turned to jelly. Her stomach twisted into knots. It was lucky she hadn't had time for breakfast that morning, or she felt certain she'd have expelled it all on the stage.

"What are you doing?" Monica's voice hissed from behind the wings. "Go!"

Someone shoved Agnes. She tottered forward, stomach still churning. What were those cues? Smile, wave, walk.

Forced a smile on her face, Agnes waved toward the back

of the stage as she beelined for her workstation. Her mouth felt dry.

Focus on the case. Focus on the case.

Marie had said that someone swiped icing from the top of Nigel's cake. But what if it was something else that had been stolen?

"On your marks, get set, bake!" a voice declared, and a flurry of activity began.

At the workstations further down the stage, Margie unwrapped butter she'd had sitting on the counter, and Sandra dumped a tub of cream cheese into her mixing bowl. Lilah banged her fist on a bag of graham crackers. And in the back, across from Agnes, Sebastian weighed a bowl of melted chocolate.

Now that the contest had begun, they'd all engrossed themselves in their own recipes. None of them glanced around to spy on carrot cake ingredients.

"Aunt Agnes, you have to start!" Fran's voice shouted from the audience.

Agnes jumped. Her limbs shook as she remembered the hundreds of eyes staring at her. She had to grip the workstation to stop from falling over.

But she did need to start baking, or at least appear like she was. Otherwise, she'd be booted off stage.

Agnes ducked behind her work station, which served the dual purpose of hiding her from the audience's eyes and allowing her to search for the items she needed. She wanted a scale for the flour, a grater for the carrots, measuring cups, and the ingredients from the fridge.

Soon the stand mixer turned the butter and sugar while Agnes grated the carrots. Nigel's cake topper had been stolen. That meant—

"What are you doing?" Esther's voice shouted from the back of the audience.

Agnes didn't need to look up to know that her boss was yelling at her. But why? She'd been measuring her flour and using the scale just like she was supposed to do.

"Use a bowl, Agnes!" Ashley called, holding back laughter. "For measurement!"

Agnes stared at the tumbling mountain of flour that she'd poured onto the scale. How was she supposed to use a bowl? That would affect the weight! Though she supposed that she could subtract it. Yes, that was it. Perhaps a bowl would be cleaner.

A bell rang, signaling the halfway point in the Bake-Off. The other contestants had already pre-heated their ovens and were sticking their creations in. While they baked, they'd make garnishes and toppings for presentation points.

The judges stepped onto the stage, as was customary at this point in the competition.

Agnes had forgotten to add the vanilla essence to her batter. She searched for the bottle and discovered that she'd grabbed almond extract instead. Close enough! She measured the teaspoon over the mixer, trying to finish before the judges reached her table.

They were talking to Lilah now, or rather listening as she spoke. Dr. Michaels smiled politely. Tobias Thornton tapped his pocket and checked his watch as he nodded along. Josephine Charles didn't even pretend to be civil: she turned her back to Lilah and dipped a long thin finger into the brownie mix. The old woman's nose wrinkled in consideration as she tasted it.

Agnes' hand slipped, and the small bottle of almond essence fell into the mix, flooding it with the flavor. But she doubted it mattered. More essence could only enhance the flavor. Then she dumped the dry ingredients into the wet. The speed of the mixer sent a cloud of flour flying back onto her face.

The judges were with Margie now. Agnes watched them from the corner of her eye.

Josephine Charles asked a few pointed questions. Dr. Michaels gratefully accepted the taste of icing presented. Tobias Thornton took a spoon as well. His left hand continued to rest on his pocket.

What has he got in there that's so important?

"My dear girl," Josephine snapped as she turned to Agnes. "Have you not put your cake in the oven yet? It will be underbaked!"

Cake batter had always tasted delightful to Agnes anyway, but she knew better than to say that. Instead, she turned off the stand mixer and poured the liquid into the nearest pan. It was only after she'd finished that she realized she'd never greased it.

But it didn't matter.

Agnes was onto something.

The killer had wanted the topper from Nigel's cake. It must have been something valuable. They could have taken it and run off, and no one would be any the wiser.

But the murderer had to still be in town.

Even if they hadn't broken into Nigel's house, they'd stolen Marshmallow.

The killer must have wanted him for a reason.

Agnes approached the ovens with the cake pan. "Don't open that oven, Agnes! My brownies are in three!" Lilah shouted, running toward her.

But it was too late.

"Sorry, Lilah," Agnes said, sliding her cake pan into the hot oven alongside the tray of brownies. She hadn't preheated any of the others earlier, and there wasn't time now.

The judges marched toward Agnes. Josephine led the way.

"My dear, your methods are highly unusual. Are you trying to sabotage your competitors?" the old woman reprimanded.

"I'm sure she's trying her best," Dr. Michaels said, taking up for Agnes. He gave her a sympathetic look. "Your batter looks great."

"No, her batter looks lumpy and uneven," Josephine objected, pointing toward what remained in the stand mixer.

"Well, I'm sure it tastes good," Dr. Michaels offered. He took a few steps toward the work station, dipped his finger into the bowl, and licked. His eyes widened and he choked out a single unconvincing word: "Delicious." Then he coughed.

Tobias Thornton barely noticed the exchange. His eyes flicked from his watch to a clock off stage. He still had his hand in his pocket.

"What've you got in there?" Agnes asked, stepping toward him.

Tobias' head jerked up. The question seemed to have caught him off guard. "Only my keys and wallet. Nothing of significance."

He was lying. Based on how the judge had been acting, Agnes was certain of two things.

First, Tobias was anxious to leave Warrenton. And second, he had something of great value that he'd recently acquired hidden in his pocket.

Agnes had a hunch that she knew what it was.

Without thinking, she lunged forward. Tobias raised his hands to block her on instinct, perhaps expecting a blow. But Agnes went for his pocket. Her fingers wrapped around a thin piece of fabric. She pulled it. Half of Marshmallow's collar slid from Tobias' pocket.

"What in the world are you doing?" Josephine pulled Agnes away from Tobias. "You're causing a scene."

It was true. Agnes had become the center of everyone's attention. Even the other bakers had paused to watch.

But Agnes didn't care about all the eyes on her, not at that moment. She felt giddy from the shock as the pieces of the mystery snapped into place.

"Tobias Thornton killed Nigel and then stole my rabbit," Agnes said.

And she knew why.

Chapter Thirty-Seven

MURDER BUNNY

I hopped out of Uncle Curtis' truck. I had to get inside and reveal the truth: Uncle Curtis had kidnapped me, and that he clearly was Nigel's murderer. Though what precisely Curtis wanted with a carrot cake recipe, I hadn't quite figured out. Perhaps the man was simply mad. He certainly acted that way, planning to keep me in a cardboard box for the rest of my life.

The absolute nerve of some people.

There were a lot of steps to get into the Robin Good-fellow Theater. Clearly, it hadn't been designed with bunnies in mind. But I had to hop to it, quickly. If Curtis had killed Nigel, he might do the same to his niece.

I was the only one who could solve the case.

I scampered up the long set of steps into the building. Luckily, no one noticed a white rabbit on the loose; their eyeballs were all inside, glued to the contest.

Inside, I scurried and leapt through the corridors until I made it to the entrance to the theater.

I arrived just in time to hear Agnes' voice. She was facing the theater and shouting at the top of her voice:

"Tobias Thornton killed Nigel and then stole my rabbit!"

I wouldn't really refer to myself as *hers*. I saw it more as a partnership of equals. Then I stopped. My whisker twitched. My eyes went wide.

Had she just said Tobias Thornton was the murderer?

That wasn't right. Or was it? I cast my eyes to the shoes of the man standing beside Agnes. Dear God, I recognized them. Those were the very shoes I'd seen sneak out of Nigel's tent after he dropped to the floor. They were the same ones that had been present during the theft of my collar. But what would he have wanted with Nigel's carrot cake recipe?

"My dear, what nonsense are you spewing?" an old woman on the stage demanded. "Mr. Thornton is a well-respected member of the art community. I invited him here myself."

Tobias laughed nervously. "It's all right, Josephine, I'm sure the girl's just suffering a breakdown from the contest."

"I'm not!" Agnes said, voice louder and bolder than I'd heard it before. Her hand dove into Tobias' pocket and she pulled out a very familiar strap of fabric.

It was my collar. The brute had brought it with him to the contest.

"This is Marshmallow's collar!" Ashley's voice shouted from her seat near the stage. I saw the sixteen-year-old stand up and point, waving to her grandmother.

Margie approached the judges. "Indeed it is."

A handsome man who I recognized as Nigel's former doctor raised an eyebrow. "How do you explain why a rabbit's collar is in your pocket, Mr. Thornton?"

"I'm sure there's a good explanation," the old woman said, but she'd turned an accusatory gaze onto Tobias.

"There is," Agnes said. "Tobias killed Nigel because he wanted to steal his cake topper. It was an antique of some kind. Sebastian, you said it looked like a church of some kind, didn't you?"

The baker in the corner looked up, horrified to be dragged into this mess. He lowered his bag of icing. "It was."

"But when the police found Nigel, the topper was missing from his cake," Agnes continued. "It must have been expensive. But I'm guessing it was worthless without this."

She lifted my collar into the air and shook it. The bell jingled, and the audience gasped. Agnes was quite the performer. I hadn't realized. She had them all eating out of her hands.

"You realized it was missing and left the Announcement Dinner early to break into Nigel's antique shop and hunt for it," Agnes said. She was laying all the facts out on the table. I of course had figured out many of them on my own, being a terrific investigator, but Agnes had gone even further than I had. "When you realized the police were investigating, you pinned the crime on Brandon Dorchester."

"I knew my baby was innocent," Lilah Dorchester interrupted, but the audience paid her no mind.

"You must have been furious when you didn't find the missing bell. Maybe you even intended to break into Nigel's house and look for it again. But then, quite by chance, you met me in the Batter Chatter. I had Nigel's old bunny with me–"

I didn't appreciate the adjective.

"--and on his collar was the very bell you'd been hoping to find. I'll bet you couldn't believe your luck. All you had to do was kidnap my bunny, remove his collar, and steal the bell. Then you could leave town and no one would be any the wiser."

Agnes had left out the part where her uncle became his accomplice, but I suppose she couldn't have learned all the facts on her own. I would fill her in later.

I caught sight of Uncle Curtis shuffling uncomfortably nearby, in the back of the theater. Judging from the surprise on his face, I don't think he'd known that Tobias was a killer. The fool had probably stolen me from his niece for an easy few dollars. I ought to rat him out to Agnes, but I'm a different species. And seeing as Tobias might've killed me without Uncle Curtis intervening, I supposed I might owe the man. I decided I'd keep his secret.

But onstage, the performance wasn't over yet. It was Tobias' turn to take the spotlight.

"This is a preposterous story," he accused, voice deep and booming. "That is the last you will be seeing of me today!"

Tobias was panicking. I could see the emotion on his face. As a creature primarily hunted as prey, I am exceptionally good at recognizing such an expression. In his fear, Tobias lunged for Agnes and ripped the collar from her hand. A woman shrieked. Then he leaped from the stage and into the audience, striding boldly through the people, who parted as he moved.

Agnes jumped after him. It was an unexpected stroke of courage from my new partner. I was proud of how far she'd come. But I'd seen Agnes run, and I'd seen Agnes try to make herself known. She'd never catch Tobias, or stop him.

Not without my assistance.

I hightailed it down one of the aisles. As a bunny, I am incredibly speedy when I need to be. And I'd had an idea.

While baking onstage, Agnes had used the carrots but discarded the carrot tops. She'd tossed them over the edge of the counter, towards the garbage can on the floor, but had missed it entirely. They were laying there on the hardwood, glistening under the lights.

I leaped onstage and hopped over to the pile of greens. I heard the audience gasp and then *awwww*. It took a moment before I realized the sounds were directed at me. True, I was used to hearing these comments, because I'm really quite adorable, but never in such quantity or volume.

There would be time to accept the praise later. Now was the time for action, as repugnant as that action might be. I jammed my face into the pile of carrot tops and opened my mouth and grabbed as many as I could. They were wilted, bitter, and slimy. I couldn't believe anybody ever touched this vegetable for fun.

But they were perfect for my purpose.

With a mouthful of carrot tops, I took a flying leap offstage and hit the floor with a thud. I heard an *ooooh* from the audience. In a flash, I scrambled back onto my four paws and streaked down the aisle towards Tobias. He was striding boldly towards the exit, nobody stopping him.

I caught up to the guilty judge, saw where his next footstep was going to land, and slid the carrot tops directly beneath the sole of his shoe.

All humans are huge to me, but Tobias is bigger than most. His foot hit the slippery greens and slid forward. His arms windmilled wildly. Soon his bulk began teetering, and in two shakes of my own tail his body was falling backwards. I squealed and slipped out of the way, darting quickly beneath a chair.

Tobias hit the floor with a thud that echoed through the theater. I heard more *ooooohs*, which made my own feel less special.

Agnes was on top of him a moment later. She was scrappier than I'd realized, pinning him with her knees and trying to fight him for my collar. I wanted it back myself, so to assist, I bit his thumb.

Tobias shouted in pain. "How did that cursed creature get here?" he demanded, loosening his grip on the collar.

Agnes' eyes locked onto mine. She seemed to notice me for the first time, and a grin spread across her face. I have to admit that we felt like a team.

The moment Tobias released my collar, Agnes grabbed it back and rolled off him.

"You silly fool," Tobias gasped, flat on his back on the floor. "You have no idea what you have there."

"Tell me," Agnes said.

"That bell was carved by the famous miniaturist Franz Jean Jacques! It's made of solid gold and the clapper is diamond. When it's in the church, the piece is worth a small fortune to the right collector. You imbeciles in this miserable podunk town have no idea of its value. And the biggest imbecile of them all was Nigel. He was using it as a cake topper! Can you imagine the disrespect! Jacques was a master! Such a piece deserves to be in better hands. Poisoning him was a public service." He paused, then looked guilty. "Whoever did it, of course."

My ears went flat. On her knees, Agnes sat back on her heels, mouth fallen open. Tobias had confessed, then tried to backpedal.

A pair of police officers ran up the walk; I'd seen them lounging in front of the theater a few minutes earlier. I recognized Officer Wilson, who'd been on the scene when Nigel had first been discovered.

"What's happening?" he said.

"Theft, burglary, and kidnapping," said Agnes. Then she added: "And likely murder as well. Arrest this man."

Tobias lifted his head, saw the police officers, and lowered his head back down to the floor. "You'll all have to help me up first."

Agnes and I and the rest of the crowd watched as the police officers crouched on either side of Tobias and hoisted him up, one arm beneath each of his armpits. Once he was on his feet, they carried him out to the corridor, where they began speaking to him.

Almost immediately, the crowd began applauding. I looked up at Agnes.

"It's for us, Marshmallow," she said.

I looked around. All I saw was a forest of shoes and pants. I lifted my head a bit higher, where I saw the smiling human faces. They were all staring at me.

Agnes slipped my collar back onto my neck. "Marshmallow, you are a magician. Who kidnapped you? How did you escape? And how did you get all the way here to the Bake-Off?"

I twitched my nose. My eyes worked back and forth.

"Okay, we'll catch up later." She looked at me adoringly. "I am so pleased to have to you back. Don't leave ever again."

I allowed her to snuggle me to her face and neck. I confess that I may even have enjoyed it, especially with the continuing cheers of the crowd.

Chapter Thirty-Eight

AGNES

For the next week, Agnes Brooms and Marshmallow became local celebrities.

A headline in the Warrenton Bugler announced the news:

MURDER BUNNY AND NEW OWNER SOLVE DEATH OF NIGEL DAVIES

Marshmallow seemed chuffed by the article. Without a word, the bunny had taken the article into his crate and had sat on it, his little eyes scanning the print left and right.

Agnes' feelings were mixed. As someone allergic to attention, she wouldn't have minded if the writer had focused only on Marshmallow. But the article had mentioned Agnes several times, and her photograph appeared at the end.

But Agnes' brief brush with celebrity pleased one person greatly: Esther. The people of Warrenton had been flocking to the library since the article's publication, asking to see the local sleuth and her rabbit. They were happy to donate a few dollars while they did. It wasn't the flood of money Esther had been hoping for, but the library had bought itself a few more months before they needed to panic again. Agnes just hoped her boss wouldn't trot her out to speak to potential donors.

"Do you need to put on sunglasses so you won't be recognized?" Cindy joked. She sat in the passenger seat of Agnes' car. There were no kids in the back, only Marshmallow. Scott had agreed to watch the kids for the day.

"Marshmallow's the real celebrity," Agnes said, climbing out of the car and getting the bunny's carrier out. "Maybe we should buy him sunglasses."

"I think that would make him stand out more." Cindy laughed, but she grew serious as they approached the Batter Chatter. "You know, I don't think I ever apologized for not believing you about Nigel's murder. You were right to be suspicious."

"I appreciate you saying that," Agnes said. "But I understand. What I was saying was tough to believe."

Agnes pushed the door open, and they stepped into the sweet-scented, pastel-coated interior of the Batter Chatter. A chime announced their entrance to the store.

Ashley rushed them at once. "Marshmallow! You're here! I've got a treat for you."

Before Agnes could object, the sixteen-year-old had pulled the bunny from his carrier and into her arms. Ashley scratched between Marshmallow's ears as she carried him to her purse and rifled around inside.

Standing near the entrance, Cindy nudged Agnes and chuckled. "You did go a bit crazy with your theories. I mean, you claimed the rabbit was communicating with you."

Both of their eyes went to the fluffy white bunny. One of his large ears flopped down. He nibbled a piece of lettuce that Ashley had handed to him. There was nothing about Marshmallow that seemed magical or hyper-intelligent at all. He was just a regular rabbit.

"I may have been imagining that," Agnes admitted.

"You think?" Cindy grinned and pulled Agnes forward. "Come on, we're here for something important, remember?"

Right on cue, Margie stepped out of the back. Sebastian followed at her heels, complaining, "I just think my eclairs should—"

"Why it's Agnes, the woman of the hour!" Margie shouted in delight, cutting off Sebastian. Beaming, the store owner walked toward Agnes and wrapped her in a bear hug. "I've been hoping you'd stop in. We owe you a huge apology. We should never have doubted you."

"I knew you were right about Nigel's death the whole time," Ashley shouted from the opposite corner where she still held Marshmallow.

Margie sent her granddaughter a look. Then she continued to beam at Agnes. "Today, take anything you want. It's on the house. You were fantastic, dear. Cornering Tobias like that. Warrenton is safer, thanks to you!"

"Has this whole town gone mad?" Sebastian demanded. He stomped his foot, rattling a shelf full of measuring implements. "She ruined the Bake-Off!"

Agnes grimaced. As nice as everyone was being, Sebastian wasn't wrong. This was the first year since the Bake-Off began that there had been no winner. Her public declaration of Tobias' guilt had distracted the participants. Lilah had already been fretting about her brownies and forgotten about her secret sauce. Margie had missed the timer on her muffins, Sandra had accidentally added salt to her strawberry cheesecake topping, and Sebastian had run out of time to finish the elaborate icing he'd planned for eclairs. Furthermore, even if they'd kept baking perfectly, thanks to Agnes, they'd lost a judge, which would've thrown everything into turmoil.

"Don't be silly," Margie said, lifting a wooden spoon from

a container nearby and wagging it at Sebastian. "Agnes is a local hero."

"She's a walking disaster," Sebastian objected. "And I'm positive she never had Nigel's carrot cake recipe."

"That is true," said Agnes, "but I was trying to solve a murder, Sebastian."

"I think she's wonderful," Cindy offered, wrapping an arm around Agnes' shoulders. "Anyway, Aggie and I are planning to have our own Bake-Off."

"You're letting her back into a kitchen?" Sebastian said. He sounded aghast.

"No, I'm taking a break from baking for a while," Agnes promised. "But Cindy and I were thinking that it might be nice to have a small party to celebrate. I thought you all could bring the goods that you would have baked for the contest, and we could all try them."

Sebastian's brow furrowed. "How would we decide the winner?"

"I don't think there'd be one," Agnes said.

"That's a splendid idea, Agnes!" Margie said. "I'd be delighted to attend. I'm sure the others will as well. And if they don't, I'll declare myself the winner by default." She winked.

Sebastian rolled his eyes, growing huffy. "I will of course attend. If it's a celebration of baked goods, I'll need to be there." He continued to eye Agnes suspiciously. "You promise you won't be making a carrot cake for the event?"

"Cross my heart," Agnes assured him.

"Then what are you here for now?" Sebastian asked.

"Snacks!" Cindy informed him. "We're having a movie night, and you can't beat the tins of cookies Margie sells here."

"But those are made in some factory somewhere," Sebastian protested.

"And they're delicious," Agnes said, pointing to a stack of cookie tins next to the cash register. "We'll take two, Margie."

Margie laughed and waved her hands. "Take them, Agnes. Whatever happened with the Bake-Off, I for one will be sleeping a lot better now that we have a certified detective in Warrenton."

"Oh, I wouldn't go that far," Agnes said, laughing off the compliment with some embarrassment.

But the comment stuck in her head as she and Cindy drove back to her house for their movie night.

Agnes Brooms had never imagined herself as a detective. But what if that was what she was about to become?

———

Early the next morning, Agnes quietly crept out of bed and descended to the kitchen. She walked on the tips of her toes. Cindy had enjoyed a few too many glasses of the wine and crashed in the living room instead of driving home. Her soft snores rose and fell from the couch.

Marshmallow lay in his carrier, curled up on his newspapers. One eye cracked open at Agnes' approach.

She smiled, pulled some spinach from the fridge drawer, and crouched before him, holding it out.

"Listen, Marshmallow," Agnes whispered. "I have to pretend to think that you're a regular rabbit, but I know better. I want to be a detective, but I can't do it on my own. I need you. Will you be my partner?"

The bunny gave her a quick nod. Agnes smiled and held her finger up against his cage. He nuzzled it with his wet nose.

NIGEL'S FAMOUS CARROT CAKE RECIPE

INGREDIENTS FOR CARROT CAKE

- 2 cups all-purpose flour (250 g)
- 2 teaspoons baking powder
- 1 teaspoon baking soda
- 1 ½ teaspoons ground cinnamon
- ½ teaspoon ground ginger
- ¼ teaspoon ground nutmeg
- ½ teaspoon salt
- ¾ cup vegetable oil (180 ml)
- 4 large eggs
- 1 ½ cups packed light brown sugar (300 grams)
- ½ cup granulated sugar (100 grams)
- ½ cup unsweetened applesauce (125 grams)
- ½ teaspoon vanilla extract
- 3 cups freshly grated carrots (300 grams)

INGREDIENTS FOR CREAM CHEESE FROSTING

- 1 8-oz package of brick style cream cheese (226 grams), softened
- ½ cup unsalted butter (115 grams), softened
- 2 cups powdered sugar (240 grams)
- 1 ½ teaspoons vanilla extract

DIRECTIONS

1. Preheat the oven to 350°F (180°C). Spray two 9-inch round cake pans with non-stick cooking spray. Line the bottom of each pan with parchment paper.

2. In a mixing bowl, whisk together the flour, baking powder, baking soda, cinnamon, ginger, nutmeg, and salt.

3. In a second mixing bowl, whisk together the oil, eggs, brown sugar, granulated sugar, applesauce, and vanilla extract. Add the grated carrots and mix until well combined.

4. Pour the wet ingredients into the dry ingredients and mix with a whisk or rubber spatula. Don't over mix.

5. Pour the cake batter evenly into both pans. Bake for 30 minutes. A toothpick inserted into the center of each one should come out clean.

6. Remove from the oven, transfer to a wire rack, and allow to cool in the pans for 20 minutes. Then remove from the pans and return the cakes to the wire rack to finish cooling.

7. Using a stand mixer or a hand-held mixer, beat the cream cheese until smooth. Add the butter and mix for 1 minute until smooth.

8. Add the powdered sugar and vanilla extract and continue mixing.

9. Level the tops of each cake with a knife or cake leveler.

Place one of the cake layers on a cake stand, top with 1/2 cup of the frosting, and smooth it out into a single layer. Then place the other cake layer on top. Apply the remaining frosting on the top and sides of the cake.

10. If desired, add chopped pecans, chopped walnuts, or other toppings.

ADDITIONAL NOTES

- This recipe can be easily adapted to a 9x13 pan or a cupcake tray.
- The applesauce may be replaced with sour cream or plain Greek yogurt.
- The frosting may be replaced with a vanilla buttercream or whipped cream frosting.
- This carrot cake will last in the refrigerator for several days, if sealed properly. It will last for a few months in the freezer.

PLOTWORKS PUBLISHING

If you enjoyed this story, please leave a review at the place where you purchased it.

Then visit Plotworks Publishing to find other stories to enjoy!

Now turn the page for a sneak peek at the next delightful Murder Bunny cozy mystery—

BOOK
2

a cozy mystery

MURDER BUNNY

and the

A spelling
bee emcee
is d-e-a-d.
Do the
sprinkles
spell
murder?

Deadly
Donut
Disaster

HANNAH DOVE

MURDER BUNNY AND THE DEADLY DONUT DISASTER

Agnes Brooms rode in the front seat of her best friend Cindy's car. A large rabbit carrier squashed her lap. Within was a fluffy white bunny she called Marshmallow. Unfortunately, Cindy's three daughters had taken up all the room in the back seat.

"You didn't need to bring the bunny," Cindy said, shaking her head in disapproval as Agnes shifted under the carrier's weight.

"He doesn't like to be left at home alone," Agnes objected. "Last time, he got into the fridge and ate all the tomatoes."

"Lock his carrier then."

"He undoes it."

Cindy rolled her eyes in disbelief, but she didn't understand his secret. Marshmallow wasn't a regular rabbit. He was a possible genius. Agnes had inherited him after the murder of her neighbor, Nigel Davies. Calling the bunny a pet would have been inaccurate. He was a full partner, and they had solved the case together.

Of course, last time she'd tried to explain this to her friends, they'd thought Agnes was losing her mind. So, she quickly added, "It's a cheap carrier, so the lock is probably broken. But I really don't have the money to buy a better one."

"Maybe you could tie it with some string," Cindy offered.

"He'll chew through—" Agnes started to explain, but was interrupted by three voices from the back of the car.

"We can hold him, Aunty Aggie!"

"Yes, let us take the bunny!"

"Please!"

Cindy's daughters, Fran, Josie, and Rebecca adored Marshmallow. Unfortunately, the feeling was not mutual. They squeezed and poked the rabbit, who definitely did not like it. Normally, Cindy took her daughters' side and pestered Agnes to let them play with the bunny. But today was different.

"No, he'll distract you," Cindy said, glancing at her kids in the rearview mirror. "Fran, you need to focus. This is a big night for you. There's a chance you could win this whole thing!"

The nationally renowned Buzzworthy Spelling Bee had been scheduled to be held in Warrenton at Fran's elementary school. As part of the deal, the children who'd done the best in their class had been invited to compete in the first round of the competition.

Cindy was over the moon. She'd already started planning how they'd celebrate when Fran brought home the trophy. She'd insisted Agnes come to the competition for moral support, and because she assumed that Agnes cared as much about her own children as Cindy did.

Agnes had agreed, but not because she saw anything fun about attending a children's spelling competition. She suspected that Cindy would need comforting when Fran inevitably got eliminated. The nine-year-old may have beaten her twenty-four classmates, but this was a national competition.

"Okay, Fran, quiz time." Agnes paused to think for a moment. "How do you spell ... disenfranchisement?"

The nine-year-old took a minute to sound it out, but she successfully spelled out all eighteen letters.

"See?" Cindy said, grinning in the front seat. "She's brilliant!"

"It has my name in it," said Fran, "of course I know how to spell it!"

Agnes was forced to agree. Secretly, she thought she should've chosen a word that wasn't phonetic.

They parked in the lot of the elementary school. She pulled her daughters out of the backseat, brushing dust and crumbs from their dresses. Agnes hefted Marshmallow's crate.

"Aunty Aggie, I don't think they'll let you bring that into our school," Josie said.

"Marshmallow can wait in the car," Cindy agreed. "We'll leave the windows down."

Agnes glanced at the bunny. He shrugged in a rather miffed way. She suspected he had as much interest in watching a children's spelling bee as she did, but it felt rude to ditch him after she'd dragged him all this way.

"Sure, sounds like a plan," Agnes said.

When Cindy and her kids weren't looking, Agnes opened the crate, pulled Marshmallow free, and snuck him into her purse. It was a large one, but he didn't quite fit. The rabbit kept his head low as they approached the entrance.

A group of parents and kids clustered around a lone security guard.

"What do you mean we can't go inside?" a father demanded, clutching the hand of his daughter. "Daisy's been prepping for this all day."

"Is the contest taking place tonight or not?" asked one of

the mothers, and the question was at once taken up by several others.

The security guard raised his hands in an effort to placate them. "Settle down, folks, would you? I'm telling you everything I know. When the police come out, you can hound them about what's happening with the spelling bee."

Agnes' ears buzzed at the mention of the police. She glanced into her purse at the hidden bunny. She could see Marshmallow's nose twitching like it did whenever he was thinking.

Cindy pushed her way forward, dragging Agnes and the kids with her. "Excuse me, we just arrived," she informed the security guard. "What's happened?"

A sudden sob came from behind the security guard. It was a young woman, her dress showing a slender figure, her blonde hair swept into a high ponytail. Not a single strand was loose, giving the sense that she usually took great care with her appearance. At present, mascara coursed down her cheeks.

"Fenton is dead," she said, sobbing out the words. "I found him on the floor in his office."

Two white ears rose from within Agnes' purse.

"I'm sorry, who is Fenton?" Cindy asked.

"He's the emcee," the woman snapped. "He ran this whole spelling bee. And all you all care about is if the contest is still happening. It's not! Go home!"

There was more muttering from the gathered parents and confused children. The woman burst into tears again, and the security guard offered her a tissue.

Slowly, the crowd began to disperse.

"This is weird," Cindy said, nudging Agnes. "We should go wait in the car until the police come out."

"You go," Agnes said. "I think I should find out more."

Cindy's brow furrowed. She gave her friend a pointed

look. "Listen, Aggie, I know you solved Nigel's murder, but you're not a detective. And this Fenton fellow might've had a heart attack for all you know. What're you sticking around for?"

Agnes hesitated. Her friend had a point.

A foot thumped Agnes from within her purse. Maybe she wasn't a detective, but Marshmallow certainly considered her to be one. And he clearly wanted to learn more as well.

"Just humor me," Agnes pressed. "I came here to support you."

"To support Fran," Cindy corrected her, but she took her kids and waved them toward the car.

Agnes hunched over her purse, pretending to search for something, so she could whisper to Marshmallow, "Stay hidden and listen!"

He sniffed. She realized that he was probably annoyed that she'd felt the need to give him such an obvious instruction.

Agnes took a deep breath and approached the security guard and crying woman. Cindy was probably right. This wasn't necessarily a mystery, and Agnes wasn't necessarily a detective. Yet, Agnes couldn't shake the feeling that she'd stumbled onto another case.

PLOTWORKS PUBLISHING

Visit Plotworks Publishing to find other great stories to enjoy!

But first, turn the page for a sneak peek at a Hannah Dove book that will turn *you* into the detective!

STEAM B⬤AT WILLIE

Vol. 1

WHISTLESTOP
PUZZLE MYSTERIES

*Seven exciting puzzles
for you to solve!*

HANNAH DOVE

STEAMBOAT WILLIE WHISTLESTOP PUZZLE MYSTERIES, VOL. 1

CASE #1: THE CAPTAIN'S GIFT

There's a lump in your throat as you walk toward the large ship docked at the end of the harbor. You wonder if your decision to become first mate on a steamboat was a bit hasty. You're the type who enjoys quiet afternoons, curled up with a book or a puzzle. Spending your days scrubbing decks, catering to demanding passengers, and tossing coal into the boilers isn't your idea of a fun job. But after what happened to your father, you need the money.

At the back of the steamboat, you recognize a large man with a red beard and a fine white hat. Captain Ewan is the one who conducted your interview. He called you a landlubber, called you a fool for applying, and then asked when you could start. It was more than a bit peculiar, and you're not quite sure what to think of him.

"Welcome aboard the SS Wilkinshire," he announces, patting your shoulder with a bit too much force as you walk up the gangplank.

You stumble forward, almost dropping the small bag that

holds your belongings. Your eyes go to the wooden planks that make up the steamboat's deck. You think you see something small and black scurry behind a barrel.

Before you can investigate, Captain Ewan puts his arm around your shoulders and forces you to walk forward. You notice that the tip of his nose is bright red and his round cheeks are flushed.

"Let me introduce you to the rest of the crew. After that, I have a gift for you." He winks at you, and you smell the whisky on his breath.

Good thing you won't be setting sail until tomorrow.

The Captain takes you below deck to the crew's quarters. "First stop is the men's room," he announces, knocking loudly before pushing a small wooden door open.

Beyond is a small cabin with a bunk bed with two narrow built in closets on either side. A small table has been squashed into the corner by the door. Two men perch on little stools before it. One is large with bright blue eyes, a black beard, and a scar across his cheek. The other resembles a mouse, with a long nose, loose brown hair, and dark, shifting eyes. A lollipop stick protrudes from the corner of his lips.

You've caught them in the middle of an argument.

"Could've at least let me help instead of making me sit in a corner and watch," the mousy one protests, lollipop stick twitching as he speaks.

Black beard snorts. "Absolutely not. I know what a sweet tooth you have. You'd have swiped some of it without a second thought, you pilfering little—"

"Ahem!" The Captain interrupts them with a loud whisky-scented cough. "Our new first mate is here. Perhaps we want to make a better introduction."

The two men stop fighting and finally notice you standing behind the Captain. You wave in greeting.

Black beard stumbles to his feet. He's so tall, he has to stoop to avoid banging his head on the ceiling. You wonder how he manages to survive on such a small boat.

"Joe Steely," Black beard introduces himself. "I'm the resident chef on the SS Wilkinshire. Honor to have you aboard." He holds out his hand, and you shake it. There's powder on his hand.

When you look down at your fingers after, you see that they've been stained with something brown.

"And I'm Biggie O'Toole," the mousy one says. He doesn't stand up, but salutes you from his stool, leaning back as much as he can in the cramped space. "Been wondering when you'd arrive. You a fan of sweets?"

His eyes flick toward the bottom bunk. There's a large glass jar with an assortment of sweets.

Your eyebrows rise.

Biggie's lips quirk upward in a smile. He takes the lollipop out of his mouth. "Figured. But don't take any of mine. Even if you is the first mate."

The Captain scolds Biggie for his rudeness and hurries you out the room.

"Don't mind Biggie. He'll warm up to you. All the crew will." He turns away and mutters under his breath, "Eventually."

The two of you visit the girls' room next. It's only a few steps further down the passage.

Captain Ewan knocks again before opening the door.

The cabin within is identical to the one you just visited. Only there's a rather unpleasant smell. You try to breathe in through your mouth, wondering if it has to do with the woman lying on the bottom bunk. She's rather large with dark hair and a forehead covered in sweat.

"Awful isn't it," a young, straw-haired blonde says, holding her nose and making a face as she steps out from behind the door. "I've had to do her job all day and care for her. She's drank so much water the river might run dry."

To prove her point, the blonde points to a cup resting precariously on the edge of the bed frame. The glass has a brown, sweat-covered smudge.

"My goodness," the Captain says. "It's food poisoning again, isn't it? Estelle, you know you aren't supposed to eat dairy." There's a concerned look in his gaze as he studies his sick crew member.

"It's Joe's fault," Estelle moans. "He probably put milk in the eggs this morning." She sits up and notices you for the first time. Her groaning stops, and suddenly, she doesn't seem quite as violently ill. "Who's this?"

"Our new first mate," the Captain introduces you to the two women. "Estelle is our cleaner, and Gertie is our errands girl. She fills in wherever she's needed."

"I prefer to think of myself as a waitress," the blonde, Gertie, informs you. "It's the most glamorous of my tasks."

You shake her hand. It's slightly damp, and smells faintly of soap.

The Captain keeps the rest of the introduction brief, probably looking for an excuse to escape the rather foul-smelling room. He takes you a few steps further toward your cabin.

There's only one bed pressed against the wall. The rest of the space is filled with a built-in dresser and small desk. It's not much larger than the crews' cabins, but at least it's clean, and you won't have to share.

Captain Ewan points to a silver box on top of your pillow. "That's a little something for you to welcome you to the team. I rested it there less than an hour ago, so it shouldn't have melted. I do hope you like it." He nods at you. "I'll leave you to settle in."

You thank him, and his cheeks turn red as though he's not used to gratitude from his crew.

Once you're alone, you drop your small bag on the desk, lift up your present, and open the box.

It's empty.

"There was a bar of chocolate in it," a small voice informs you.

A shiver tickles the back of your neck. Your eyes dart around the room. There's no one else with you.

Could it be a ghost?

"Psst, down here."

You follow the sound of the voice to the foot of the bed. Something small and black scurries onto your sheets until it stops on your pillow.

Your eyes grow wide.

Sitting on your bed, grinning up at you is a mouse, dressed in a yellow rain jacket and holding a piece of cheese. He crosses his legs, leans back on your pillow just like a human, and continues to talk.

"Who are you?" you ask.

"Name's Steamboat Willie," the mouse replies. "I've been on this ship for the past year, so I know all about how things work. Crew is full of thieves, every whistlestop brings some disaster, and more than a few people have died aboard. I'll bet Captain Ewan left all that out when he offered you the job. But don't feel bad. Now you know the truth, you can run along and quit and leave me in my room in peace." He closes his eyes, wiggling his butt against your pillow.

When he opens them, he sees you still standing in the room.

"Huh? Why aren't you running? Are you slow?" he asks, giving you a puzzled look. "The last few first mates bolted the moment they heard me, but you don't seem terrified of a talking mouse. Maybe you're different. Tell you what, I'll let you share my room if you can pass my test. Think you're up for it?"

You shrug.

———

Which of your new crewmates stole the chocolate?

    a. Joe
    b. Biggie
    c. Estelle
    d. Gertie

If you need a hint, turn to the back of this book.
If you know the culprit, turn the page for the solution.

PLOTWORKS PUBLISHING

Turn the page to find another Hannah Dove title! This story is aimed at anybody who feels the irresistible tug of family and home—

GIRL
seeking
FARM

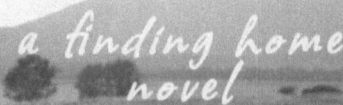

a finding home
novel

It's been
waiting for her
all this time.

HANNAH DOVE

GIRL SEEKING FARM

Jessica stepped to the curb at the small airport, dragging a pair of heavy duffle bags and a fabric suitcase. She smelled the air.

It smelled rich and humid. Like home.

A white Ford F150 was approaching her. It was spattered with mud around the bottom edges and sported mud flaps behind the rear wheels. Jessica cocked her head. She hadn't seen a vehicle like this in a long time.

It pulled to a stop. The driver's door opened, and a tall, gangly man stepped out. He was wearing a simple plaid shirt, jeans, and a pair of well-worn work boots. His face was broad and his high cheekbones looked sharp enough to open cans. His face said trustworthy.

"Young Billy," she said. "It is *so good* to see you."

"Likewise, kiddo." Young Billy wrapped his long arms around her and gave her a long squeeze. It felt better and lasted longer than any hug she had ever received in the city. "Nonna is real excited to see you. That's all she's talked about for the last two weeks."

He bent down, lifted her bags, and easily tossed them into the bed of the truck.

"There is some breakable stuff in there," she said.

"Sorry, darling," said Young Billy. "The pigs aren't quite as sensitive."

She climbed into the passenger seat of the cab. It was clean. In the dashboard was a satellite radio.

Young Billy eased the car out of the pickup zone and onto the freeway. When they'd left the airport far behind, he finally exhaled. "Congestion makes me get all worked up. I need my elbow room. Coffee?"

He gestured to the cup holder, where a paper cup was waiting.

"For me?"

"Of course. I brewed it this morning."

Jessica smelled it. "Drip coffee?"

"Oh. Let me guess. You probably like espresso now."

Young Billy was right—there had been a mandatory cappuccino break every morning at *Spretza*—but Jessica decided it was better not to admit that. She replaced the paper cup back in the holder. "I'm okay for now."

Young Billy reached forward to the satellite radio. "It's goin' to be a long drive, and I'm not much for talkin', so we'd better put some music on."

He hit the power button, and the sounds of lap-steel guitar exploded out of the speakers. He immediately turned it down. "Sorry. I like it kinda loud when I'm by myself."

She listened to the music for a while. In perfectly clear enunciation, the singer was complaining that he couldn't ever get drunk enough to forget his problems. Jessica hadn't heard any music like this in a long time. In New York City, she'd only listened to Dutch electronic beats, which were challenging. This music, though, was neither. It was exactly what you expected, exactly what you wanted.

"What do you think?" said Young Billy.

"Of what?"

"The music."

"It's not my favorite."

"This is Blake Shelton. He's my favorite. He's got a really good voice."

She shrugged. "It's okay, I guess."

"Stay out here for a while, and you'll come to like it."

The truck rolled off the highway, turned west, and headed out into the rolling fields. Jessica's stomach rose and fell as the vehicle floated up and down the gentle crests and troughs.

Young Billy rolled down the windows. "Let's get some fresh air in here. You probably haven't smelled this in a while."

Jessica inhaled deeply. The smell of clover, of pine, of earth filled her nostrils. It was alluring.

"That smells great," she said.

"You can't get tired of it," said Young Billy. "So, there's something I should probably tell you about."

"What's that?"

"There've been some changes at the farm recently. We sold the Holsteins."

She nodded. "Nonna told me last year."

"No more dairy. The new regulations were impossible. We just got out completely. It's easier this way."

For a moment, Jessica lost herself in nostalgia. During her two years on the farm, she'd been assigned the job of milking the family's three dairy cows. It'd been strange at first, squatting on the stool, squeezing the teats, but she'd quickly grown used to it. Of course there'd been plenty of modern equipment that could have done the task, but with only three cows, Nonna had said it was unnecessary. Mostly, she hadn't wanted to invest in the machinery, not when your granddaughter would do it for free. In New York, Jessica had noticed that people tended to stare, then burst into laughter, when she admitted to knowing how to milk a cow, so eventually she'd stopped talking about it.

Soon the land flattened out, and Jessica felt a stab in her heart as she recognized the local general store.

Hackmore's.

It'd been done up like a big red barn, even though it was a normal concrete structure underneath. She was glad to see that it had stayed the same. The big sliding front doors were still in place. The bales of hay out front. It still even had the adorably hick sign, a man in overalls with a hayseed in his teeth.

"Good to see some things don't change," she said.

"That's not exactly true," said Young Billy. "Hackmore's goin' through some rough times. The old man died last year, and his kid doesn't want to keep it open."

"Why?"

"The corporate farms don't buy so much as a single seed there. They got their own distributor for everything." He shook his head. "Hackmore's is antiquated. It's from another time."

"I remember playing on the sacks inside when I was little."

Young Billy smiled. "I played on those sacks too. Don't get me wrong, we buy from them when we can, because I'd hate to see them close. Jesus, I'd have to drive sixty-five extra miles, one way, just to get a few extra bags of feed."

A few miles later, the plains were broken by a stand of trees that ran parallel with the road. Alongside the trees, about thirty meters in, was a creek.

Jessica craned her head. "The creek hasn't changed either. Still tiny."

"When those thunderstorms roll through," he said, "you better stay the hell away from that creek."

"I remember," she said.

He suddenly grew serious. "No, it's *worse* than you remember."

"What do you mean?"

"I don't know why the weather has changed, but everything's real screwy now. Every year for the last six years, that creek floods higher and more often than before. Last year it ruined Kilkenny's soy crop."

Jessica remembered how Kilkenny's property was at least a hundred meters away from the creek. "That's pretty scary," she said.

He nodded. "You'd better believe it. Personally, though, I think it would take an act of God for flood waters to touch Nonna's toes. And if they tried, she'd probably point her finger and tell that dirty water to jump right back to wherever it came from."

Jessica laughed. Feared but respected, her grandmother was not a personality to be taken lightly.

As Young Billy slowed the truck, Jessica felt her heartbeat speed up. There, on the right, was the familiar long deer fence—actually two fences, about a foot apart, to discourage jumping.

Then the driveway appeared. The simple sign hadn't changed: *Nonna's Farms*.

Jessica felt the warmth spread like syrup through her body, first in her thighs, then up into her chest and down into her feet. If there was any place on earth that needed to stay the same, this was it. And Nonna was making sure of that.

Young Billy cranked the wheel of the truck, and they rumbled down the dirt road, the bare springtime fields on either side, towards a distant structure.

Nonna's house.

PLOTWORKS PUBLISHING

Be sure to visit our store at Plotworks Publishing to discover even more titles to enjoy!